The
McBays
At Autumn's
Crossing

Bob Self

LIGHT SWITCH
PRESS

The McBays at Autumn's Crossing
By
Bob Self
Watch for my third book in the series,

"The McBays Ace Angel Comes to Town "

Published by:
Light Switch Press
PO Box 272847
Fort Collins, CO 80527

Copyright © 2018
ISBN: 978-1-949563-14-6
Printed in the United States of America

DEDICATION

I dedicate this book, my second book The McBays at Autumn's Crossing, to Karen, my wonderful and supportive wife of fifty-one years. To my always helpful, loving daughter, Autumn, and to my compassionate and strong grandson, Dakota, whom I am so proud of for his daily strength.

INDEX

Chapter 1
Cheyenne Meets the McBays

Cheyenne's long strawberry blond hair was blowing in the breeze. Cheyenne had a cowboy hat sitting on the back of her head plus boots about knee high. She had jeans on that fit her like socks on a turkey. Meaning the jeans must have been cut just for her figure. Also, Cheyenne had on a white shirt with the top two buttons unbuttoned.

As everyone else was climbing down from their horses and wagon seats, they noticed the eye contact of KaSandra and Cheyenne. KaSandra and Cheyenne could have passed for beautiful twins. They both had jeans on that fit their hour glass shape, also white shirts, boots and cowboy hats sitting on the back of their heads. KaSandra had her long blonde hair blowing in the breeze and Cheyenne had her long strawberry blonde hair blowing in the breeze. It looked like a standoff, with neither one moving.

But then KaSandra and Cheyenne both climbed down from their horses and hugged and said how glad they were to finally meet. Then everyone else hugged Cheyenne and then it was Shermons turn. Shermon hugged Cheyenne and they kissed for what seemed like a full minute. But after the kiss Shermon said. Cheyenne McBay, sounds pretty good don't you think so? Cheyenne asked Shermon, are you asking me to marry you? Shermon said, yes, I am, if you will have me. Cheyenne said, Well I think Cheyenne Decker-McBay, sounds pretty good. Shermon and Cheyenne kissed again, and everybody was fighting back happy tears.

Cheyenne asked Shermon, when do you want to tie the knot or get married, I mean. Shermon said, why not in a year. We will have time to plan and get ready for a Waco wedding if that's okay with you? Cheyenne agreed, that would be great. Everyone hugged again and even Kid, Wes Montana and Harry Austin joined in with hugs and slaps on the back. After a little while Wes told Shermon, me and Harry will be back in a little while and they rode off.

Chapter 2
The McBays Check out an Old Shack

Shermon said, there is an old shack about 200 yards from here. Also, there is a lake maybe 5 or 6 acres in size with a creek running in one end and a small stream running out the far end. I believe the lake and stream will be a great water source and the shack we could use while building our ranch house. We could always burn the old shack later. Reminton said, well let's go see what it looks like.

But when the women seen the old building they fell in love with it. KaSandra said, Shermon, I don't think we will burn this building. Reminton and Wyatt also said, they thought the old building had a great deal of possibilities. Lance said, Sherm looks like the structure is good and maybe later it would make a great bunkhouse for wrangler's. Shermon said, well let's give that some thought. Plus, I guess we could rework that large slant roof shelter for horses if we wanted too. Shermon said, well let's unhook the oxen and picket the remuda over in that clover after we water them. KaSandra said, let us sweep this place out before bringing anything inside.

Blue was growling and barking towards some rocks. Reminton and Dakota walked over to where Blue was barking. Blue was barking at a large rattle snake. The snake was coiled and ready to strike. Reminton pulled his gun and started to shoot it. Dakota said, don't shoot it, I want it! Reminton said that snake is poisonous, and the venom will kill you if it bites you. Dakota said, I will be careful Uncle Rem. I heard that the meat is good and then the skin would be good for hat bands and more. So, this snake is worth a lot of money. Dakota lifted the snake with his rifle barrel and put it in a wood crate. Reminton said, you be careful, Dakota and walked over to where Shermon was looking at the old corral.

Shermon said I guess we should tear this old corral down and replace it with a new one as soon as possible. Reminton said, yes, I guess we will need a large corral and maybe two before we are done. Lance and Wyatt walked over, and Lance said, me and Wyatt have some good ideals for the old place here. Shermon said, that's good and I think we should make some plans in the morning.

Shermon said we have the three wagons close to the shack or as the women call it the old homestead and soon to be the bunkhouse. In the morning we can unload the remaining dry goods and everything else and maybe put all the tools in the small wagon for now. I think it would be a good ideal to keep the small wagon, so it could be used for a chuck wagon later. We will sell the two large wagons and all the five oxen later.

KaSandra said, you need to see this place now that we have cleaned it up some. Abigail said, I think you men could make this place real nice if you wanted too. Lance said, I think you're right Abigail. Brandy said, the coffee is ready, and we will make something to eat, but we need to make some kind of table first.

Cheyenne said, Kid and Harry should be back so could we wait a little longer then eat? Shermon said, I guess we could wait but what about a table? Cheyenne said, they are bringing a table with them. Reminton said, hear they come now. Wes Montana and Harry Austin was pulling a flat wagon back. There was a table at least 10 feet long and 4 or 5 long benches on the flatbed wagon. The large table could stay 10 feet long or be two 5-foot-long tables because the table had double legs in the middle. So, there was 8 legs on the 10-foot table. Shermon said, this is a real nice table, but we will have to get use to sitting at a table again. Wes said, that it was his and Harry's gift to Shermon and his family. Cheyenne said, they also brought back some food so let's eat.

They set up the 10-foot-long table plus there was two tables on the porch of the old place. KaSandra said, there was more than enough table space. Cheyenne asked, Kid and Harry to unload the food. Shermon said, that is the biggest ham I have ever seen. Cheyenne said, there is white potatoes, corn on the cob, dressing, plus onions, tomatoes, peppers and of course, biscuits. KaSandra said, we have tea and of course hot black coffee. Shermon said, I would like to thank God for my family and our friends plus this great meal. They all said amen and then ate.

Chapter 3
The group sits around and talks after a great meal

They all agreed how good the meal was and how good it felt to be sitting at the large table. Reminton said, you know I can't remember how long it has been since I had ham. Everyone agreed how good the ham tasted. Wes said, on the other end of town there is a couple that raises hogs. Harry said, yea, but they can't bring any in town unless it is dead and ready to be cooked. Shermon said, like the town folk, I don't care to smell them pigs.

Then Shermon said, it looks like there is a need for some good beef here in this town? Harry said, yea, there is the pig farm and a small chicken farm, but a good steak is pretty costly. Dakota asked, Lexi if she wanted to go with him to catch another rattle snake and Lexi, said, yea. It wasn't long Blue was growling and Wyatt yelled, Dakota, you and Lexi be careful!

KaSandra said, who wants more coffee and she asked Reminton to bring the large coffee pot over to the 10-foot table. Cheyenne said, it's getting late, maybe I should head back to town. KaSandra said, Cheyenne, if you want to stay, you can bunk in that old place with us women. Cheyenne said, she thought she would stay. Shermon said, Kid you and Harry can throw a bedroll down under the stars with us if you two would like too. Kid, Wes Montana, and Harry Austin both said they would like to stay. Cheyenne told Kasandra,

I will try not to ask too many questions, but I will stay tonight. KaSandra said, Cheyenne, you can ask all the questions that you want to because I would like to ask a couple questions myself.

Shermon poured some coffee in Wes Montana's cup and asked, Kid when do you think you and Harry will be ready to move to Autumn's Crossing? Wes said, well me and Harry both work for Cheyenne and a small rancher, but we already told the old man that we would be moving here as soon as you were ready for us. Harry's son, Mario, also works there with a couple other good hands, but the old man is going north as soon as he can. Shermon said, Kid I would like to talk to those other good hands, if you think we can use them. Then Shermon said, Harry, I would like to talk with your son Mario and see if he would want to move out here and live at the ranch then I would consider hiring him on.

Shermon said, well I'm ready for a little shut eye, how about you fellows? Reminton said, yea, I could sleep some. Lance said, the three girls want to sleep in one of the wagons and I told them I thougt it would be okay. Shermon said, well there's three wagons, so I guess it would be fine. Dakota said, well the four women are giggling too much for me, so me and Logon will be out here with you men. Shermon said, well pick a place you two cowboys. Reminton said, I am sure that there are no snakes in those wagons, but I can't guarantee there is none on the ground. Dakota and Logon both said how about we take this first wagon because the three girls are already in the second wagon.

Shermon smiled and said, I'm sure that the snakes are over in those rocks, but if you two fellows want to sleep in a wagon go ahead. Shermon said, well let's throw out our bedrolls and get some shuteye. Shermon then said, Hey, Kid, I want to tell you and Harry both thanks again for all you two did for me and my family. Wes Montana said. Shermon, me and Harry both were glad that we could help.

KaSandra, Cheyenne, Abigail and Brandy all four, came to the door and said goodnight, the girls were sleeping, and Dakota and Logon were almost asleep. Shermon said, we will see you all in the morning, sleep well.

As the four women laid down, KaSandra asked Cheyenne, how did you and Shermon meet? Cheyenne said, well these two cowpokes got the drop on me. Then a large man in buckskins said, as cool as ever. I believe you two better turn that lady loose. KaSandra said, that sounds like our Shermon.

Cheyenne said, it was. But then they messed up, because they said, why don't you make us. The one guy was hanging on to me with one hand and the top step with his other hand. Shermon stomped so hard on that guys hand that the guy screamed out loud. The big smelly guy let me go to grab his hand. Shermon came with a right that broke big smellie's nose, then hit him in the chest and the guys eyes went crossed. Then Shermon hit him with an upper cut that lifted him off his feet and when his feet hit the ground again he was out cold.

The other guy came at Shermon and Shermon had a spoke from a busted wagon wheel that Shermon hit the guy with on both sides of his face. What a mess… The guys nose was broken, and his jaw was broken, also half of his teeth had been knocked out and he was trying to tell Shermon he was done. Then Shermon looked at the other guy who also said it's over for now. Shemon said, "I won't tolerate rude people!" Then we went and had lunch and we talked for hours. I didn't want to let Shermon leave because I knew I had found the man for me. KaSandra said, that was the same way when I met Reminton, I knew I had found my man.

Cheyenne said, but I have to say I have never seen a man put a beating on another man the way Shermon puts a beating on a man. KaSandra said, I know what you mean. Shermon does fight to win and he does win. I have seen him and when he whips a man that man stays whipped for a long time. Cheyenne said, Shermon said, he whipped those two men to save my honor and then said it's over now, but I might have to kill them both later and I will if they force me too. But for now, it is over.

KaSandra then told of the two men in Eldorado that Shermon beat so bad for grabbing her and then told them he would kill them if he seen them again and you could tell he meant it. Brandy told of the Navajos how Shermon charged them before the apaches showed up to help. KaSandra said, we all knew Shermon blamed himself for the Navajo's attacking our small wagon train, plus everything else that happened. Like you asked about the gunfight. Well Shermon sat on the front line with Wes Montana and Harry Austin but he would have sat there by himself if possible. Shermon did everything he could to keep the gunfight from us.

Shermon was glad that Wes, and Harry were there but he felt it was his fight and he wanted to end it without any of us getting hurt or even involved in the gunplay. There was Zach Reams and three other gunslingers sitting in front of Shermon, Wes and Harry. Two had split off to the left and two had split off to the right. Anyway, Lance and Wyatt were going up through the trees on one side and Reminton was heading up through the trees on the other side. The rest of us were ready with our guns in camp.

Zach Reams the gunslinger, and three of his gunhands were shot down by Shermon, Wes and Harry on the front line. But there were four others making there way towards our camp. They were coming through the trees as Lance, Wyatt and Reminton was heading towards them. Lance got wounded, but he and Wyatt both killed one of Zach Reams saddle tramps and Reminton had also killed one, plus, Dakota and Logon killed one. Except, there was one more and he had Reminton in his sights when KaSandra dropped the gunman with two shots to his chest. Cheyenne said, good for you KaSandra.

Then KaSandra told how Lexi Lee's dad had been killed and now she was with them. Cheyenne said, I cannot believe all that you have been through together. Plus, I heard you all met a tornado head on. Cheyenne said, that proves how close of a family you really are. KaSandra said, Cheyenne there was some bad times but there sure was some good times on the trail also. Well I sure am glad you all made it, said Cheyenne. KaSandra said, so are we and like Shermon said it will make us a better family in the long run.

Cheyenne then asked about Shermon's capture and said I just can't imagine how anyone could endure all the pain. Cheyenne said, Wes Montana mentioned it, but did not say much. KaSandra said, Shermon said he thought of us, his family, and that kept him going.Cheyenne said, Wes mentioned that Shermon had many whipping marks on him. KaSandra said, yes, he does have, but she thought that Shermon might want to tell Cheyenne himself.

KaSandra asked, I wonder how long Abigail and Brandy have been sleeping? Cheyenne said, I don't know but I'm feeling tired, aren't you? KaSandra said, yes, I am, but Im sure glad we had this talk. Cheyenne said, me to, see you in the morning sleep good on your first night off the trail. KaSandra said I will but first I need to thank God again.

They both prayed and thanked God for their Family and friends.

Chapter 4
The McBays go to town

The next morning Shermon asked, who wants to go to town? Cheyenne said, I would like to take you all to meet Micka and Daniel Grant, they own the general store. Shermon said, that's a great ideal. Then Shermon asked, what can you tell me about that lumber mill outside of town? Cheyenne said, that saw mill that you seen on your way here is owned by Rick Adams. They call him "Lucky" and he is a real nice fellow. Shermon said, that's good because we are going to need more than a little lumber and it looks like he coud use the business. Cheyenne said, before talking to Lucky, I would like you to meet Marshal Mountain, Mitch Smith and his deputy Ringo.

Shermon said, okay but why do they call the Marshall "Mountain Mitch"? Cheyenne said, because Mountain Mitch is almost seven feet tall. Shermon said, well that sure is a big Marshall! Then Shermon asked Cheyenne if her, Wes and Harry would mind meeting him and his family in town. Cheyenne said, they would be happy too. Shermon said, let Mountain Mitch know we will see him real soon Cheyenne, and thanks. Cheyenne stopped by the marshalls and told him of Shermon and his family.

Shermon looked at his family and said, we are here and there is a lot to do, but I want to do it as a family. Reminton asked, what do you have in mind Sherm? Shermon then said, we have over $15,000.00 of our homestead money, plus the wagon ad oxen to be sold later, right? Reminton and a couple others said thats right. Shermon said, we will be fine. I know we all have money of our own, but I would like everyone to keep their money separate and use it for personal things or really things that are not part of our horse ranch, if you know what I mean, Shermon asked? Reminton and the rest said, that they did understand what Shermon meant and that as fine.

Then Shermon said, I know that there is a large party of us, but I think that it would do the town good to know that not only there is quite a few of us now that stand together as a family but also, we are here to be there friends as well, if given the chance. Shermon Asked, are you ready to go see the Marshall, Mountain Mitch? Reminton said, do you think we should take at least one wagon with us for dry goods? Shermon said, lets take one so whoever wants to ride in a wagon can.

Valerie let out a big breath of air when she knew she would be in the wagon. She was not ready to try a horse. Shermon knew Valerie was afraid of horses, but also knew in time she would lose her fear of horses, but it would be in her own time. Shermon asked, how many horses do we need to saddle? Reminton said, you will be on Buck, so I guess seven other horses. Lexi said, I would like to ride my horse, blackie, if that's okay? Shermon said, of course, Lexi. KaSandra said, Reminton you know which horse I want, will you get it for me, while we make a list of drygoods? Reminton said, I sure will. So, let me see, Reminton said, Buck, Blackie and the one KaSandra likes and then I guess five other horses.

So, after the wagon was hooked up to two oxen and there were 8 horses saddled Shermon said, are we ready for town? Plus, Shermon said, I hope the town is ready for us! Shermon said to Reminton, this is a wonderful sight us all heading to town together. Reminton looked around and said, it sure is Sherm, smiling from ear to ear.

So, Abigail said, to Logon, Katelyn and Velerie, grab Blue and get comfortable. Shermon said, let's roll to town, as he buckled his two colt .44's on his hips, and Reminton did the same with his colts. Shermon looked at KaSandra who had a .44 on one side and a large bowie on her other side fastened around her small waist and riding low on her hips. Shermon said, KaSandra we don't want to shoot anyone, unless we must, and smiled. KaSandra said, Sherm I wont shoot anyone unless I must, and smiled back.

Shermon said, let's go see Marshall, Mitch Smith first then we can go to the general store and meet the owners. Shermon said, Abigail, pull the wagon in front of the general store, as eight horses were tied to the wagon. Then they all stood with Shermon as Mountain Mitch stepped out onto the boardwalk. Shermon said, my name is Shermon McBay and this is my family. The Marshall extended his hand to Shermon and said, I'm Marshall, Smith and they call me Mountain Mitch. The marshall said, hi, to all the McBays and they all said, hi back.

The Marshall said, I see a lot of guns, why so many? Are you expecting trouble? Shermon said, we do have quite a few guns with us, but we are not looking for trouble. But if trouble finds us we need to be ready. We have found pretty much trouble on the trail and we were ready so that helped us. The Marshall said, yea, Cheyenne mentioned some, but Shermon if we get a chance I would like to hear more. Shermon said, Marshall, I will be happy to tell you more later after we get settled in some. The Marshall said, Shermon, my friends call me Mountain Mitch, and I know you have a lot to do and if I can help let me know. Shermon said, I will see you soon, Mountain Mitch.

Shermon said, well let's go see what the general store has and meet Micka and Daniel Grant. Then I would like to go by the sawmill and talk with Rick Adams. Micka was sweeping the boardwalk out front of the general store when the McBays all walked up and Micka said, I bet you are the McBays. Cheyenne told me you all were coming. Daniel Grant then walked out and said, Hi and they all shook hands. Shermon said, lets get enough for a few days and then come back for more, Okay?

Chapter 5
The Sawmill is for sale

They all agree to get maybe enough for two weeks. Cheyenne walked up and said to the Grants, I see you have met the McBays. Then Wes Montana rode up and said to Shermon I'm meeting Harry at Potter's Café, but I just heard Lucky Adams is looking to sell the sawmill. Shermon said, do you know why? Or for how much? Wes said, No, but I heard he wants to leave town, he is getting to old to run a sawmill. Shermon said, well I will have to go by and see Lucky Adams as soon as I get done here. Shermon said, thanks Kid, and tell Harry I said Hi also, will you? Wes Monstana said, I sure will Sherm and me and Harry will be out to see you later.

Shermon then turned his attention to Micka Grant. Shermon said, me and my family would like to do a lot of business with your general store. But first, I would like to see your inventory on your guns, ammo and leather goods. Micka said, we have more dry goods and household goods, and not much on ammo and tack and the like. Shermon said, that's good, I would like to talk with you about that. Micka Grant said, he would like to. Shermon said, Okay, why don't you show me what you have while the women put together a list of supplies to take back with us. Micka showed Shermon a few guns he had with a small amount of ammo. Then he showed Shermon a saddle, a few bits and braces and a couple latigo's.

Shermon said, within 2 weeks there will be at least 20 people staying at Autumn's Crossing, our ranch, and more to come later. We are going to have a large horse ranch and will need a lot of weekly and monthly supplies. Micka said, that's good, Shermon, do you want me to keep more ammo or leather goods on hand. Shermon said, Micka I would like you to keep very little on hand. Micka said, what you mean Shermon? Shermon said, Micka with all the extra supplies we will be purchasing from you I'm sure you will double your sales on supplies. But we will have a gunshop and a blacksmith shop plus we will work on guns and sell all leather and tack items plus ammo at Autumn' Crossing, our ranch.

Micka said, So, Shermon, are you telling me that you don't want me to sell any guns, ammo or leather items. Shermon said, What I am saying is we will be in full operation soon! Selling and working on guns and saddles and tack, plus we will be looking at buying the saw mill.

Shermon said, if you sell a gun or ammo or tack I have no problem with that but I am willing to buy most of what you have on hand at this time and if you decide not to carry guns, ammo and leather items that will be your choice but I can promise you that you will need all the shelves you have for other supplies that you will be selling to our horse ranch at Autumn's Crossing.

Then Daniel Grant said, Shermon, you said that we would at least double our sales in just supplies. Shermon said, that's right! Daniel asked Micka, what are you waiting for you know we don't want to sell guns or ammo anyway. Micka said, Okay, Shermon, Let's do it! Shermon said, Okay, box up the guns, ammo and tack and we will pay you a fair price. Micka and Shermon shook hands, then came to a price for the guns, ammo and leather goods. Shermon paid the Grants for it all, plus a wagon load of other supplies. Shermon said, we will need more supplies in 2 weeks. Will you be able to take care of us? Micka and Daniel at the same time said, you bet we will!

Shermon said, well whoever wants to head back to Autumn's Crossing can, but whowever wants to go with me to buy a sawmill, let's go! Reminton said, Shermon, if you and Wyatt and Lance want to go to the sawmill I will head back to our future horse ranch with the rest and help get our supplies in the building you called an old shack. Shermon said, if that's what you want to do. We will go talk to Rick Adams about the sawmill and see what he would want to sell out for. KaSandra said, Shermon when you three get back we will have some food ready, and black coffee. Cheyenne said, Shermon, I will be out later. I have a couple things to check on. Shermon said, see you soon and kissed her.

Chapter 6
The Marshall gets shot

Reminton and the rest head out of town leaving Shermon, Lance and Wyatt talking with Mountain, Mitch Smith in the Marshalls office. Shermon told the Marshall of his dealings with the Grants and that they were going to see Rick Adams about the mill. The Marshall said, that he looked in on Rick Adams, about him selling the sawmill. The Marshall said that "Lucky", Rick Adams, was getting up in years and Lucky's wife had died about 2 years ago and he had let the sawmill get in bad shape. Shermon asked the marshall if he knew what Rick Adams plans were? Mountain Mitch said, that Lucky had some family up north somewhere and they asked Lucky to come live with them. Also, that he did not think it would take much for the McBays to acquire the sawmill. Shermon said thanks, Mitch, and shook his hand and the three McBays headed for the sawmill.

As Shermon, Lance and Wyatt reached the sawmill they heard a lot of shooting back at town. Shermon told Rick Adams they would be back and the three McBays headed back to town. When the three McBays reached town, they seen the Marshall laying in the street and there was a man standing over him getting ready to shoot the Marshall again. Shermon pulled his .44 and shot the guy twice in his chest. There was shooting at the back of the bank and the Marshall yelled, that's Ringo, my deputy, Shermon can you help him. Wyatt said, Shermon I will stay with the Marshall.

So Shermon and Lance started towards the back of the bank as the towns doctor came to help the Marshall. Wyatt went through the front door of the bank as Shermon and Lancce reached the back where the deputy was shooting it out with two of the bank robbers. Shermon told the two to drop their guns or meet their maker. Just then Wyatt came through the back door and one of the bank robbers shot him. Wyatt went down as Shermon shot and killed the two bank robbers. Lance ran over to Wyatt, but Wyatt was already pulling himself up. Wyatt just got nicked, Lance yelled.

The deputy had his gun on Wyatt, and Shermon said, hold on Ringo, that's my brother. Ringo said, and who are you? Lance said, we are the McBays and the Marshall is in the street out front. He's been shot. Shermon said, we came to help so let's go out front and see the Marshall. They all walked around the front, but the deputy still had his gun on Shermon.

Marshall Smith was sitting up and told Ringo to put his gun away before Shermon or one of his brothers shot him. Ringo said, Okay, but who are these cowboys? Shermon was checking Wyatt out and said, I'll be. Wyatt said, what? Shermon said, Wyatt you just couldn't stand me being the only one missing a piece of ear! Lance looked and said, Wyatt now you have a piece of your ear shot off just like Shermon and laughed out loud.

Ringo asked the doctor, James Cain, if the Marshall was okay? The Doctor said, we need to get the Marshall over to my office and get the bullet out. Wyatt bent over and with Lance's help he carried the Marshall over to the doctor's office. Before leaving the doctor's office, Shermon filled Ringo, the deputy in as quickly as possible about him and his family. Then Shermon said, you did good Ringo. Ringo told Shermon, you and your brothers saved the banks money, not me. Shermon said Ringo we were glad to help, but you did good. Shermon said, we will stop back later to see how the Marshall is doing. Now we are going to see Rick Admas. Ringo said, well you must hurry because Lucky is leaving and going to live with his family up North. Shermon shook hands with Ringo and told him they were going to see Lucky about the sawmill. Ringo said, thanks for the help and he knew for sure there would be reward money for saving the banks money. Shermon said, give it to Doctor Cain, and smiled at the Doctor.

Chapter 7
The McBays buy the Sawmill

While Shermon, Lance and Wyatt headed for the sawmill, Cheyenne heard about the gunfight and headed for Autumn's Crossing. Cheyenne road into the ranch full speed ahead and seen Reminton and yelled, Reminton, Where's Shermon? Reminton asked, whats wrong? Shermon, Lance and Wyatt went to see Rick Adams. Cheyenne said, where is Brandy? Wyatt's been shot. Reminton called for Brandy and asked, again how did it happen as he was mounting his horse. Cheyenne said the bank was being robbed and Shermon, Lance and Wyatt, all three got in a gunfight with the robbers. Brandy and KaSandra was on the front porch now and Brandy asked, you said, Wyatt was shot by a bank robber? Cheyenne said, Yea, I believe he is okay, but take my horse, he is saddled, and I will wait for you to get back. Reminton told KaSandra that he and Brandy would be back soon and rode off. Then Cheyenne told KaSandra and Abigail, let's get out of this sun and, I will tell you what I heard.

As Reminton and Brandy headed to town, Cheyenne told everyone else what she knew about the bank being robbed, and about the shootout that Shermon, Lance and Wyatt were in. She told them that the Marshall was shot and so was Wyatt, but she thought they both were okay. Reminton and Brandy stopped off at the doctor's office and Doctor Cain told them that the Marshall did not make it. The Bullet was lodged in to deep and the Marshall bled out while he was trying to save him. Brandy and Reminton said, they were sorry about the Marshall but was also concerned about Wyatt. Doctor Cain told Brandy that Wyatt was okay and was even laughing because now he had an ear like his brother, Shermon's.

Reminton said, Brandy let's ride out to the mill. On the way to the saw-mill, Reminton said, here comes Shermon, Lance and Wyatt now. Brandy rode up and checked Wyatt's ear and then kissed him and told Wyatt, Lance and Shermon how happy she was that they were okay. Shermon said, yea, things could have been worse. Reminton said, I guess it was bad for the Marshall, because he did not make it. Shermon said, I will be back at Autumn's Crossing soon. I think I will stop by the doctor's office and then go see Ringo.

Shermon said, first before heading back, tell everyone about the deal we made at the sawmill. Lance said, Sherm that can wait until you get back from town and I will stay with you if you want me too. Shermon said, no that is okay. I will be back soon and let Cheyenne know also. Lance said, see you soon Sherm.

Then Shermon headed to the Doctor's office and Lance, Wyatt and Brandy headed to Autumn's Crossing. But, Reminton stayed back in town with Sher-mon. When they pulled up to the soon to be horse ranch. Cheyenne, Lexi and the rest of the McBays were waiting for news from Lance, Wyatt and Brandy. First, they all looked at Wyatt's gun shot wound and said it looked just like Shermons ear now. Wyatt said, he knew it did and now he knows how sher-mons ear must have burned him when he was shot. Brandy said, Wyatt let's go in and take care of your ear. Cheyenne and KaSandra wanted details of what happened in town.

Lance told the Story as best he could about the Marshall being shot and killed. Also, about Wyatt walking out the back of the bank, and getting shot and said how lucky Wyatt had been because Sherm had both his guns out and shot the two bank robbers dead in the street before they could shoot again. After telling the story in town, Lance, told Cheyenne that Shermon stayed in town to see the Doctor and to talk with Ringo Star, the deputy. Abigail said, what about Reminton? Lance said he decided to stay back in town also in case there was anymore trouble and Shermon might need his help.

Cheyenne asked, Lance, did you all have a chance to talk with "Lucky" Rick Adams about the sawmill? Yes, we did, Lance said, I think we made a real great deal with Rick Adams, but I will let Shermon tell everyone about the deal we made when he returns. Then Cheyenne said, KaSandra, I hate to be asking so many questions but Shermon told me, if I had a question just to ask any one of his family, so I have another question? KaSandra said, Cheyenne, you are part of this family or will be real soon, so ask away. Well, Cheyenne asked, why, Autumn's Crossing? What I mean is where did the name Autumn's Crossing, start?

KaSandra said, Cheyenne, Ma McBay, always talked of Autumn the most beautiful time of the year. That Autumn was between Summer and winter and the beginning of new and good things to come. So, Autumn is something great. Like the sun setting or rising. And as far as crossing. Crossing is the crossing of streets and rivers to be crossed and connects the streets and rivers to the main place which is a wide cross area where decisions are to be made. Cheyenne said, Ma McBay was a woman that she would have loved to know and that she must have been a very great person. Yes, she was KaSandra said, so we all agreed to name our new place Autumn's Crossing. Because of Ma McBay and what Autumn's Crossing would mean to us all. Thank you, KaSandra for telling me the reason for the name you all decided to name your horse ranch and then Cheyenne said, how could you name it anything else?

Chapter 8
Shermon and Reminton arrive back at Autumn's Crossing

As Shermon and Reminton rode up to the hitching rail everyone was there to meet them and started asking questions. Shermon said, hold on a minute let us get in the shade and if we can coffee would be good and maybe a biscuit or two. So, the whole group started to sit down under the dinning tarp. As Wes Montana, Harry Austin and Mario, Harry's son, rode in.

Wes said, Shermon we heard the bank was robbed and you guys were in a shootout and the Marshall was killed. Shermon said, Wes you guys pull up a chair and have a biscuit with us and I will tell everyone what took place today. There was smoked ham, beans, potatoes, green onions, biscuits with coffee and sassafras tea. There was sixteen people all under the dinner tarp or on the small porch and after shaking hands and KaSandra saying a prayer Shermon said, lets eat then I will tell of todays events.

After having a great meal and clearing up the mess of the meal Shermon said, as you know the Marshall was killed and Wyatt was nicked, lucky I guess, but I'm not sure that Wyatt isn't a little bit happy now that his ear matches mine. Wes looked at Wyatt's ear and then he looked at Shermon's and said, well I'll be they surely match, don't they?

So, Harry Austin said, Shermon us three plus other men from town was out looking for a mountain lion that killed a dog and almost got a little girl. Wes said, yea, Sherm sorry we missed the gun play. But we heard that you got all three bank robbers. Harry said, I'm sorry also that we were not in town to help and that the Marshall got killed. He was a good man.

Wes said, we talked with Ringo and Ringo thought the bank robbers were drifters and they knew most of us were away from town. So, they tried the bank hold up and because of you they met their maker. Harry said, well the Marshall like I said, was a good man and I am glad you guys were in town to stop the town from loosing the banks money.Shermon said, he was glad to help and asked if they thought Ringo would become the new Marshall?

Wes said, I don't think he wants to be the Marshall, but he likes being the deputy. Reminton said, hey Kid, why don't you run for Marshall? Wes said, I don't want the job either I have work to do right here, right Shermon? Shermon said, that's right kid, and with Lance and Wyatt and Reminton being as busy as their going to be I will need you and Harry as soon as you are ready to move to Autumn's Crossing, so we can start rounding up horses.

How about tomorrow Wes said, we can start tomorrow if that's okay, Sherm? Shermon said, okay. Then he said we made a great deal on the towns sawmill. Rick Adams wants to go North and has lost all interest in the sawmill since his wife died a couple years ago. Rick said, if we gave him a wagon and 2 oxen that we could send him $3,000.00 in two years. There is a small wagon train pulling out in about 4 days and Rick wants to leave with them. Wyatt said, Shermon that is a great deal for that sawmill.

Shermon asked, Wyatt, how long do you think it would take to be sawing logs? Wyatt said, well there is quite a lot of work that needs to be done. But if I had a few men that wanted to work, maybe only 4 or 5 days to be milling lumber. Shermon said, you will have the men. I would like to start building in a week. Shermon said, also I would like to bring some mustangs to Autumn's Crossing within two weeks.

Then Shermon said, Wes this is where you and Harry start. I would like you two to hang a few flyers in town and let them know we are looking for a few cowboys plus a few carpenters. Shermon said, we need a horse corral or two, plus shelters. I also want 4 or 5 cowboys to go with us as we wrangle wild mustangs and any stray unbranded cows. We will pay monthly, plus found for the cowboys. Shermon said, Kid, how's $60,00 a month, plus found? Wes

Montana said, For what Sherm? Shermon said, Kid, I want you to be my fore-man here at Autumn's Crossing. Are you okay with that?

Wes Montana, said sure Sherm, if it is okay with your brothers? Shermon said, Wes they will be busy with other projects. Kid, Shermon said, I will need you to take charge of all the cowboys out on the range and the cowboys here at Autumn's Crossing. There will be plenty of times when we will be in two different places. Tell the experienced cowboys they will get $50.00 a month, plus found, they will earn it. Tell the carpenters, they will get $30.00 a month and their afternoon meal everyday they work. The carpenters will start at 8 in the morning at the mill or at the ranch and work until 5 every evening 6 days a week, plus will receive lunch 6 days a week. If they work all day their lunch will be furnished, they will earn it.

We will have a table set up for the cowboys and a table set up for the carpenters this Saturday at 8 in the morning. If they are hired they will start Monday morning at 8 and their pay will be in 30 days. Kid, Shermon Said, tell them they are interviewing for a job and to be on time or not to come. Kid said, Okay, Sherm, me and Harry is heading to town and we will have men here Saturday morning at 8. Shermon said, 8 in the morning or not at all.

Shermon told Reminton lets get a wagon and two oxen then we can get a $3,000.00 note at the bank also, for Rick Adams. Cheyenne rode in as Sher-mon and Reminton hooked up the wagon. Cheyenne asked, Shermon and Reminton if they were heading to town, and if her and KaSandra was invited to go with them? Shermon said, sure come along with us. Cheyenne said, let me go see KaSandra.

Pretty soon Lance was talking with Shermon and Reminton about the old horse corral and the shelter that stood at the backside of the corral. Shermon said, he thought they should tear it all down and start new. But then he told Lance, but I will let you decide on part or if you want all the shelter torn down. Shermon said, Reminton what is keeping those two women? Reminton said, there they are I will help KaSandra with her horse. Reminton and KaSandra went to get KaSandras favorite horse.

Shermon said, Cheyenne, you and KaSandra almost look like twins. Cheyenne said, Sherm, is that okay? Of Course, Shermon Said, I wouldn't want it any other way. Cheyenne said, I wouldn't either, But Sherm I must tell you something. What is it? Asked, Shermon. Well, Cheyenne said, you know Ringo Star wants to be the deputy and him and the town would like to see

Earl Scott become the new town Marshall, but Jack Jennings "JJ" is running agianst him and he has some cowboys behind him that want "JJ" to become the Marshall. Shermon said, well let's go see Rick Adams and then we will go see Ringo and the two men running for town Marshall. Remington and KaSandra rode up to Shermon and Cheyenne. KaSandra said, Well, are we going?

Remington said, Shermon would you look at these two women? Cheyenne and KaSandra had jeans on that fit their long legs and small wiast like socks on a turkey. Plus, they both had white shirts on and their long hair was blowing in the breeze. Sherm Said, Reminton you are right, we are a couple of lucky guys. Both women grinned from ear to ear and said let's go, when you cowboys are ready. They all smiled all the way to town.

When they reached town Shermon said, there sure is a lot of people in town today. As they reached the saloon there was a wolf whistle from a couple of the cowboys. Then someone yelled let me show you how a real man can make a woman feel. That's all it took, Shermon took buck right into the crowd of men. Shermon dove off buck, right into the big man with the big mouth and cracked him up side his head with his rifle. Shermon swung his rifle and took another guy out that was moving in on him. Shermon kicked a cowboy in his knee and as he was going down Shermon busted the cowboys jaw.

Reminton had both guns pulled and held back three cowboys that tried to move in on Shermon from the back. That left only the big man with the big mouth. And he told his men to hold back and he would teach this youngster a lesson. Shermon squared off with the big man and they unbuckled their guns. As Shermon went to hang his guns on the hitching rail the big man charged Shermon and got Shermon in a bear hug and Shermon felt the strenghth of the big man who was at least 10 years older and 50 pounds heavier than Shermon. Shermon struggled to get free but at first couldn't. Then Shermon stomped on the big man's foot, that loosened the grip enough to where Shermon had room to work. Shermon brought his head up under the big guys chin and then Shermon hit him in his big stomach with a left and then a right. The guy gasped for air as Shermon brought up an upper cut that connected solid. The guy stepped back then Shermon threw a right hook and then a hard left to the guys jaw. The guy was still gasping for air when he threw his hands up. Shermon buckled his guns on and said, I won't tolerate rude people!!

The big man said, I'm Jack Jennings and I will be running for the Marshalls Job and you will be sorry when I win. Shermon said, you haven't won yet and me and my family will be on Earl Scott's side to win the Marshall's job. Then Shermon told Reminton that he could put his guns away and thanks.

When they reached the sawmill with the wagon and two oxen they called to Rick Adams. Rick had already gathered items that he wanted to load into the wagon. Rick told Shermon that he was not concerned with the $3,000.00 note but he really wanted to get to his family. Shermon said, $3,000.00 was a very good price for the mill even with the work it needed. Shermon said, the water barrel had just been filled at the spring at Autumn's Crossing. KaSandra was telling Reminton how much she liked the large paddle wheel in the water that was attached to the sawmill. Reminton told KaSandra that the paddle wheel was what generated the power to the sawmill. Cheyenne said, well like KaSandra said, I also have stopped before just to watch the paddlewheel turn.

Chapter 9
Earl Scott is Elected Marshall

Shermon said, lets head back to town to check on the election. KaSandra asked what about that Jack Jennings, Sherm? Cheyenne said, don't you think Jennings will be wanting to try and finish the fight? Shermon said, I don't think he will try until after the election, but I will be ready for him if he does.

When they got back to town there was no Jack Jennings in town. So, the election went real smooth, because all the votes went to Earl Scott. There were a few cowboys or Jack Jennings friends that wanted to vote for Jack Jennings but his name was never put in for the election, so the new Marshall was Marshall Scott. The saloon was open but most of the friends of Jack Jennings just drifted out of town and wondered where Jack Jennings had gone.

Cheyenne and KaSandra headed for the general store and Shermon and Reminton met with Marshall Scott and Deputy Ringo. After about an hour, Cheyenne and KaSandra was crossing the street to where Shermon and Reminton was when about 5 riders were riding into town and they had Jack Jennings body with them, anyway what was left of his body. The cowboys had found Jennings body about 1 mile from town. His body had been bit more than once plus you could see teeth marks on his head and deep claw marks on his face and chest. Shermon said, Well Marshall looks like your first Marshall job has just arrived.

Marshall Scott said, Shermon, do you want to ride with me. Shermon said, sure, it's on my way back to Autumn's Crossing anyway. When the Marshall, Shermon, Reminton, Cheyenne and KaSandra all reached the site of the mountain lion attack on Jennings you could see where Jennings had been lying under cover. There were 7 or 8 cigarette butts on the ground and a half a bottle of rot gut whiskey on the rock that Jennings had been hiding behind. Reminton said, Shermon, looks like Jennings was waiting to ambush someone. KaSandra said, but it looks like the mountain lion got him before he could ambush anyone.

Then Marshall Scott asked, Shermon, this is the way you and your family travel to town and back to your ranch isn't it? Shermon said, good work Marshall. Reminton said, Sherm, with the whipping you gave Jennings, I would say Jennings was more than just a little unhappy with you. Shermon then said, well Marshall I think you should let the town know what you found here. We will head to Autumn's Crossing and check on everyone there.

The Marshall shook hands with Shermon and Reminton and said, I sure am glad that we are on the same side Shermon. You and your family be safe. As they reached Autumn's Crossing Shermon could see that everyone was a little on edge. Lance told Shermon that they had seen a large lion out by the old corral. Wyatt said, we put blue on a leash, so he wouldn't chase the lion. Shermon said, I don't think Blue would chase the lion, but I m sure that Blue would want to protect us if he could. Shermon said, lets walk over that way.

Shermon, Reminton and Lance walked out past the corral and there were large mountain lion tracks at the corral, then the tracks headed off away from them. Reminton asked, do you want to follow the cat? Shermon said, no, he would be waiting for that, let's wait for him to come back tonight. Lance said, do you think he will Sherm? Shermon, said yes, I do!

So Shermon and his three brothers waited for the cat to come back, but he never did show. Shermon said, it is a couple hours passed sundown so let's split the watch. Me and Wyatt, will watch for the cat and Reminton you and Lance relieve us in a couple hours, Okay? Shermon said, lets put our backs to the shack and watch the corral and that open area over there, Wyatt. After a couple hours Reminton and Lance relieved Shermon and Wyatt. Reminton asked did you see anything? Shermon said, no we didn't but stay alert there is a real good chance of the lion being back before morning. That morning the horses were restless, and Blue had growled some, but they never did see the lion.

Chapter 10
They Hire Cowboys and Carpenters

The McBays finish a great breakfast then set up a couple tables in the shade. The first table Shermon and Reminton sat at then the second table Lance and Wyatt sat at. The first cowboys to ride in to Autumns Crossing was Wes Montana, Harry Austin, with Mario Austin right behind them. Shermon said, you cowboys are a little early, but I like that. Want some coffee Kid? Wes Montana and Harry said, sure at about the same time. Then Harry said, Sherm this here is Mario and Sherm and Mario shook hands. Sherm said, nice hand shake, Mario. Mario said, you to Mr. McBay. Shermon said, you can call me Shermon or Sherm as my friends call me. Mario said, Sherm you can call me Mario or Mars as my friends call me. Shermon said, Okay, Mars, what are you good at or what do you like to do? Mario said, I am fast with a gun and I am very good with a rope, but I am also a good carpenter. But I prefer cowboy work when I can, Mario said.

Shermon said, good as he stood up he drew his gun and shot a small limb off a stump about 20 yards away and as he put his gun back in his holster, Mario had drawn his gun and shot off the small end of the limb still on the stump. Shermon said, Mars, that was real good shooting. But have you ever shot a man. Mario said, not yet, but I will if I have too. Shermon said, let me see you use that rope on your saddle horn. Mario made a loop and threw it around his horse's head and called his horse, Trigger and as Trigger ran by

Mario took two steps and was on the horses back they jumped the large stump and headed back. Shermon said, Mars, that was good, I know you put a lot of work into that. I will tell you, I think you are a little young. Mario said, I am a man, I am 19 years old and I will do the work of any man. Shermon said, Mars, I believe you will. How about you, starting off with Lance and Wyatt at the mill then when it's up and running you can start with the building here at Autumn's Crossing and then stay on as a ranch hand. The pay for a man is $50.00 a month and found.

Mario asked, where do I sign? Shermon placed a book in front of Mario and said right here Mars. Shermon said, sign your full name on the 3rd line. Mario signed, Mario "Mars" Austin, then shook Shermon's and Wes Montana's hand then walked over and shook his dads' hand and said I won't let you down dad. Harry said, Mario, I know you won't son. Then Mario shook Lance, Wyatt's and Reminton's hands. Shermon said, here comes some more hands. Shermon said let's start a line here.

The first cowboy was Sundance Reid, who wore 2 colt .44's in worn holsters. Shermon said, looks like you've pulled them .44's a few times. Sundance said, I know how to use them, plus, I'm real good with a rope and a horse. Shermon said sign here under Mario's name. Then Shermon said, we will have a bunkhouse soon, but for a little while you will have to roll out your bed roll under the stars. Sundance said, I like the stars. Shermon said, $50.00 a month and found. Shermon hired 3 other cowboys or horse wranglers after Sundance. Blacky Moore, Nevada Smith and Luther Green, each at $50.00 a month and found.

Then for work at the sawmill and ranch he hired Shorty Davis, Sam Reitcher, Jesse Ladrue and Shane Madison. Shermon told Shorty, Sam, Jesse and Shane that they would be working at the sawmill plus they might be at the Ranch later building sleeping quarters at the main ranch house if they worked out and were happy. They would start work at 8 every morning until 5 every evening and the McBays would provide lunch and $30.00 a month until their work was done at the end of the building or if they departed company sooner. 6 days a week, 8 hours each day, less 1-hour lunchtime each day and no work on Sundays. Sign here if you want the job.

Shermon noticed an older fellow standing back aways. His name was Cap. George Preston and he told Shermon that he used to run a chuckwagon for William Handcock but about a year ago the Indians stormed their cattle and them. The Indians drove off all the cattle and left everyone for dead. Cap said, only myself and Mr. Handcock escaped. But William Handcock is crippled, and he can't ride a horse any more. Shermon said, can you climb on a wagon seat and drive a wagon? I can, and I can shoot a gun and cook at the same time. Cap, George Preston, said, so you bet I can. Shermon said, well if you can cook and ride a wagon seat and still shoot you got a job. It's $30.00 a month and found, sign here Cap.

Shermon said, tomorrow I want you Reminton, Kid and Harry, plus Cap to stay at Autumn's Crossing. The rest of us will meet at the sawmill, then Harry you and Cap bring us some grub at noon. Cap make a meal like you would if we were on a cattle trail. They all shook hands and Shermon said, who ever needed to go to town tonight, go ahead. But tomorrow meet at the sawmill at 8 in the morning. Shermon his 3 brothers, Wes Montana, Harry Austin, Harry's son, Mario and Cap sad down with the large coffee pot. Reminton said, so where do we start tomorrow? Shermon said, we will grow this ranch pretty fast, but I never want to leave it without three or four or more men with guns ready at all times. Better to be safe than sorry.

Chapter 11
They have their men hired
— Cowboys and Carpenters

Shermon, Lance and Wyatt reached the mill at about 6 in the morning to look around a little before the other men arrived at 8 or a little before. Shermon told Lance and Wyatt that he was going to talk to Cap again about the trail drive that he and Handcock did not finish. Shermon said, there was over one thousand head of cattle on that drive, plus a Remuda of horses. There's a big demand for beef in Eldorado and no one has gone after the beef yet. Shermon said, I would like to bring some back to Autumn's Crossing, plus drive some to Eldorado to market. I don't know how many head is out there for the taking but I would think theres' a lot.

Lance I would like you and Wyatt to start on Autumn's Crossing. Build a large ranch house and turn the old place that is there now into a bunkhouse. Add to it to make it what we need it to be. We will need a couple large corrals and horse leanto's. We will start with this now and add buildings later like a blacksmith shop and gun room and so forth. The other men arrived at the mill.

Shane drew his gun and fired fast, it was a large rattle snake. Shermon walked over to the snake and picked it up with his large bowie knife then Shermon said, good shooting, how are you on a horse? Shane said, I grew up riding a horse. Shermon said, okay, if you want the job you will be trail driver and later range rider for $50.00 a month and found? Shane said, that is better than the $30.00 and found, I will take it!

Lance, Wyatt, Shorty, Sam and Jesse started the cleanup of the mill. Shermon said, that he and Shane were headed back to Autumn's Crossing with Sundance. Blacky, Nevada and Luther. I will have Cap bring you fellows some lunch later and I will see you around five or a little after. Let Shorty, Sam and Jesse go home for the night and have them back at 8 in the morning tomorrow and work on the sawmill again. Shermon and his five cowboys headed to Autumn's Crossing.

Then Shermon called Wes Montana, Harry Austin, Mario Austin and Reminton over. Shermon said, I have an ideal about going after those cows that William Handcock left. Shermon said, Reminton will you go get Cap and ask him to join us under the large dinner tarp. Reminton said, sure What's up? Shermon said, ask KaSandra to bring the coffee pot and maybe a dozen tin cups I have something to go over and would like everyone's input on my ideal.

Reminton came back with Cap and then Cheyenne and KaSandra had the large coffee pot and a box of tin cups. Behind them were Abigail, Brandy, Logan, Lexi, Katelyn, Valerie and Dakota, plus even Blue was there. Shermon said, everyone, get comfortable. Then Shermon asked, Cap what do you think about driving a chuckwagon and some of us go after them cows that you and Mr. Handcock left behind. Cap said, I always wondered why no one did go after them cows. I'm sure there is a lot of cows real close by just for the taking. Shermon said, how long has it been since you talked with William Handcock? Cap said, maybe a month, he's been drinking a lot. Shermon said, okay, there will be a list of names on the front of that wagon in about one hour. Whoever's name is on that list will be going with me to get the cows and take them to Eldorado to be sold. Then you cowboys will start earning your pay.

Reminton, I would like you and Harry to stay at Autumn's Crossing while I'm gone. Remember there's a bad mountain lion still on the loose. You guys keep everyone safe and be very careful. Harry asked, how long do you think you will be gone? Shermon said, Well I want to gather all the cows that I can and also, we might pick up a few horses on the trail. We will drive the cows to Eldorado, there is a big demand for cows there plus we might sell a few horses that we don't want to keep and bring back to Autumn's Crossing. Reminton said, we will be working on a large horse corral and shelter for the horses. Shermon said, let me work on this list of names.

Shermon wrote a list, and the names were:

Shermon

Kid Montana – Trail Boss

Sundance Reid

Blacky Moore

Nevada Smith

Luther Green

Shane Madison

Cap George Preston – Chuckwagon

These eight will leave at sunup, tomorrow morning. I believe we will be gone three weeks maybe four. Pickup Twenty-Five Dollars each from me before you leave tonight, be back by sunup tomorrow. Anyone not here will be left at Autumn's Crossing. You will be paid your remaining Twenty-Five dollars when we arrive back at Autumn's Crossing said, Shermon. Reminton, you Harry Austin and Mario Austin will remain at the ranch until we return. Of course, you will also have Dakota and Logon to help if needed. Then Shermon tacked the list of names on the wagon.

As everyone gathered around to see if their name was on the list, Shermon said, tonight you cowboys gather your gear. Bedrolls, Rain slickers and make sure you have your weapon and canteen. The chuckwagon will have extra water and ammo. Luther said, can I bring my guitar, Sherm? Shermon said, sure, there will be room in the chuckwagon for it, where you won't have to carry it behind your saddle, if you like. On the trail you will take your orders from, Wes Montana, the same as me. Anyone who does not finish the drive will not receive their final pay. Mario said, I thought that I would get to go on the round up, Shermon? Well, Mars, I will need you to stay here this trip if you will? Later, I would like you to range ride the same as Shane will do. When we return we will need at least 2 range riders when we start bringing in Horses. Okay, Mario said, that sounds good Sherm!

Then Shermon went in and got the cash box and him and Reminton sat down at the table. As Shermon gave the cowboys there start, Reminton had them sign for it. Told them that he would see them in the morning. Then Sundance, Blacky, Luther and Shane rode out towards town to gather their gear. Shermon called Cap over and started to hand him Fifteen dollars, but Cap said give me my pay when we get back. I will have earned it then. Then Cap said, I will need a helper to load the wagon, Mr. McBay. Shermon said, what about the trail, can you handle it. Cap said, I can handle the trail, no problem. Shermon asked, Logon and Dakota to help Cap, George Preston. Then Shermon asked, Mario to fill the water barrel and to get three hundred rounds of ammo from KaSandra, all 44 longs.

Okay, Reminton, Shermon said, we started with Fifteen Thousand dollars, in the cash box did you deduct the start pay? Reminton said, I gave Kid Thirty dollars and then I gave Twenty-Five dollars each, to Sundance, Blacky, Nevada, Luther and to Shane, that's One Hundred Fifty-Five dollars. No one else was in the pay line, so I deducted the One hundred Fifty-Five dollars from the Fifteen Thousand Dollars, and that leaves Fourteen Thousand, Eight hundred Forty-Five dollars. So, the final pay with Logon's Twenty dollars, would be Five hundred Fifty dollars. That's not bad Five hundred Fifty dollars a month, which it could change month to month. Shermon said, Reminton, have Logon come and see me, will you? Sure, Sherm, said Reminton. Logon came up and Shermon said, take a seat cowboy. Logon smiled and sat down. Shermon said, Logon, you are on the payroll starting now. Your pay will be Twenty dollars a month and it will go up as you do more, okay? Logon said, yea, thanks, Uncle Sherm! Then Shermon said, have Dakota and Lexi come see me, will you? When Dakota and Lexi sat down, Shermon said, you two are a part of this ranch also and someday you will share in the profits like the rest of us, just like sharing the work. But for now, if you wrangle snakes or not, I will work you both in later, if you like?

Chapter 12
They Pull Out to Take Beef Cattle to Eldorado

Cap was sitting on the wagon seat of the chuckwagon and there were seven men on horses. The sun was starting to rise. Shermon had talked with everyone at Autumn's Crossing. Shermon said, that there is a lot of cattle wating for the taking, plus the price would be Twenty-Five dollars to Thirty dollars a head. Shermon said, we will take as many to market as possible, also bring some back to the ranch. There will be Mustangs to start our horse ranch with. You know there is a mean lion out there, so be very careful. Reminton said, Sherm, we will all keep our guards up. Then Reminton said, Sherm, you be careful and keep your guard up also. They all shook hands and Shermon lifted Cheyenne up on Buck and kissed her. Shermon said, I hope to be back in 3 weeks, but it could be 4 weeks. Shermon looked around at his cowboys and, also at Cap. Then he said, Let's Roll and waved as he rode off on Buck. Everyone at Autumn's Crossing watched until they were out of sight.

So, Lance, Wyatt and Reminton with their six other men decided to start milling lumber and to replace the old horse corral and then lay out the main house and try to have it built when the eight horse wranglers pulled back into Autumn's Crossing. The men at the sawmill were going to cut some fence post logs and some split rails for the horse corral first and then have Jesse Ladrue bring the wagon load of lumber back to Autumn's Crossing and stay with Reminton, Harry, Mario and Logon. Jesse had some building under his belt. He was in charge of building the 24-room hotel in town plus the bank and a couple other buildings in the past. Reminton had asked for Jesse to be on the building crew. Reminton had Mario, Harry and Logon help them take down the old horse corral and they stacked it in a large teepee shape burn pile. Reminton said, that large burn pile will come in handy later.

Reminton said, lets lay out a large horse corral with two smaller corrals, plus a shoot for single animals. They were just about to finish laying out the corrals when Jesse pulled into Autumn's crossing with a large load of post and rails. Jesse said, you guys aren't fooling around! I can't believe you four are ready to drop post already. Reminton said, glad to see you Jesse, but I think we will eat lunch before we start dropping post in holes. Jesse said, that sounds good to me.

Abigail and Brandy said, here is lunch, as Cheyenne and KaSandra loaded lunch up for the men at the sawmill. Reminton said, you two stay alert and watch for that lion. Cheyenne said, if we see him Reminton we will skin him and bring the hide back to you. Reminton said, well just be careful and kissed KaSandra. While eating lunch Reminton said, that he would like two of the men to drop post and two to hang rails. I will work on gates for the corrals and a drop gate for the shoot, said Reminton.

After lunch Reminton started laying out one large gate facing the entrance of Autumn's Crossing and another smaller one on the back side of the horse corral. That would open into a smaller fenced in area that will be attached to the black smith shop, at a later time, Reminton told Jesse. Mario was dropping the post in the ground and Logon was feeding split rail fence boards to Jesse and Harry.

Cheyenne and KaSandra rode into Autumn's Crossing and asked how it was going. Then Reminton asked, how are they doing at the mill. KaSandra said, pretty good I think, they had quite a few split rail fence boards stacked, and Lance said, they will bring a wagon load with them when they return to Autumn's Crossing later. That's good Reminton said, we should use up all we have here today and be ready for the other load to start on in the morning. Cheyenne said, you cowboys are building a nice horse corral and I know that Shermon will be bringing something back with him to stick in that corral.

Cheyene then said, while me and KaSandra was loading up to come back there was three people that rode into town. They were with the two wagon's that left town 4 days ago. It was one man and two boys. His wife and third son were killed, also, Rick Adams was killed. Reminton said, what happened? KaSandra said, all we really know is that Shermon and his six cowboys with Cap Preston, saved these three. Some Indians had attacked, Rick Adams and Gary O'Neal and his family. Shermon and the rest of the cowboys charged the Indians and drove the live Indians away. The Indians attacked the two wagons and when Shermon and the rest heard the shooting they charged in on the Indians and they killed a couple of the Indians and the rest of the Indians ran off. Mr. O'Neal's wife was dead, and his oldest son died in Mr. O'Neal's arms. Shermon was with Rick Adams when he died. Then they buried Rick Adams and Mr. O'Neal's wife and son. That's all we know other than Gary O'Neal had said that Shermon and his men already had some cows and a couple of wild horses with them. So, as I said, I know Shermon will have something to put in that corral when he returns.

Reminton said, well, I'm sorry to hear about Rick Adams and Mr. O'Neals wife and son. Harry then said, yea I hate to hear about Rick Adams and Mr. O'Neal's wife and son, but I'm glad that Shermon and Kid was there to save the other three. Then Reminton said, we'll lets see if we can use up the rest of these fence rails.

Cheyenne and KaSandra walked away from the horse corral, KaSandra said, you know Cheyenne, I didn't even think about Indians and the like. Cheyenne said, well the farther away from town they get the more they will have to be on their guard, but Shermon has some mighty good cowboys with him and the way I see it, there's eight men out there that will be ready for whatever comes their way.

Reminton asked Harry to help him with the large double gate and for Mario, Logon and Jesse to finish up the last of the split rails that they had. Reminton looked up and Lance and Wyatt were pulling into Autumn's Crossing with a very large load of split rail fence boards. They had their two horses tied to the back of the wagon and Lance and Wyatt both were riding on the wagon seat. Harry asked Lance to pull the wagon over to where they had run out of split rail fence boards. They climbed off the wagon seat and led their ox to the water with there two horses. The girls had the coffee pot on the table with some food. Reminton said, Jesse you might as well wash up and stay for supper. Jesse agreed to it.

So, there were fourteen people sitting around and while they ate they talked about what they would do tomorrow. After supper they cleaned up the mess and then Reminton said, as Shermon would say, Lets get some shut eye. Lance said, yea it will be a big day tomorrow so who is on first watch? Jesse said, well if you's don't mind, I will stay and take first watch. Reminton said, that's fine Jesse, but there is plenty of us and I know I heard that mountain lion out there when we were eating, so I think we should double the guard through the night. Harry said, I heard it also, but I did not want to say anything in front of the kids. Lance said, Harry the women and the kids know that lion is around, so, we all need to be ready at all times, but more at night. So, I will take first watch with Jesse. Harry said, me and Mario will relieve you and Jesse in a couple of hours. Reminton said, okay me and Wyatt will take the third night watch. But even though we have a double guard everyone needs to stay alert and to keep their guard up also. Cheyenne said, me and KaSandra will be on guard inside with Blue, so don't worry about any of us on the inside. But you cowboys be careful.

That night they all heard the mountain lion kill something not to far from Autumn's Crossing. The next morning, they all sat around with black coffee and a good breakfast. Lance and Wyatt had the two oxen hooked to the empty wagon and said they would work on milling some large timbers and beams for the main house. Reminton said that he thought they would maybe finish the corral today, but he did not think they could get any farther than that, but if they did they would try to lay out the area for the main house. Lance and Wyatt headed to the sawmill and when they got there, Shorty Davis and Sam Reitcher was already there, and they were drinking a cup of coffee.

Wyatt looked around and noticed the whole area was a lot cleaner than how they had left it yesterday. Shorty said, him and Sam had got there a little early, so they swept up a little. Lance said, well it did not go unnoticed and thanked them. Shorty said, we are ready when ever you are, Wyatt said, let's fill that wagon. Sam asked, what are we milling today? Wyatt said, we need to cut as many large beams and post as possible. We can stack what we cut off the beams to be used later. As they cut the beams, they stacked them on the wagon as Wyatt suggested. Wyatt said, here they come with lunch, let's wash up for lunch. After lunch Wyatt said, let's stack some more beams on the wagon, but we need to leave enough room for post. We want the post on top, so we can take them off first. Wyatt later said, we'll the wagon is full, and it is quitting time. Lance said, we will see you two in the morning to Shorty and Sam. Lance then said, let's head to Autumn's Crossing it's getting a little late.

As they pulled into Autumn's Crossing Lance said, they have been busy here. Look at that large corral and them three horse shelters, all they need is some roofing and they will be ready. Wyatt said, I really like that shoot that leads from the large corral to the smaller one. Lance and Wyatt climbed down from the wagon seat and told Reminton that the corral really looked good, but they also liked the three shelters. Reminton said, yea all we need is some boards for the roof and they will be done. Then Reminton said, it looks like you guys have been busy, that sure is a load of beams and post you have there. Wyatt said, we cut what we thought you would need. Reminton said, let Mario and Logon take the oxen and your horses to the water and then we will have some supper and we can discuss the beams we will need.

Reminton, Lance, Wyatt and Mario washed up and were having a cup of coffee when Lance asked, where Jesse was, and Mario said, Jesse was over by the spring looking at rocks to throw under the beam post for foundation. Lance said, he didn't go by himself, did he? Mario said, No, Harry went with him. About that time, they heard shots over by the spring and then they seen Logon riding back with Harry and Jesse, behind him. As the three rode in, Reminton asked, what was the shooting about? Jesse told them me and Harry was looking at the nice supply of rocks when that Mountain Lion had snuck up behind us. If it wasn't for Logon here that cat might have had one of us for supper. Reminton said, well that cat is either awful brave or awful hungry, or both. So, we had better be careful. Logon said, I was shooting to scare the cat off, he was sneaking up on either Harry or Jesse. I wasn't for sure which one and I didn't not have a good shot, so I just unloaded a couple shots in his directions, but I didn't hit him. Wyatt asked, should we go and hunt that mountain lion? Reminton said, I don't think so Wyatt, I think we should keep our guard up and always be ready. What does everyone else think? They all agreed to keep working, but also be careful of the cat.

Then they had a good supper and Reminton pulled out some drawings he had on the main house and asked Lance and Wyatt what they thought. As Reminton rolled out the drawings he told them that it started out as an old sketch. Reminton said, Shermon had him add the five bedrooms on the back of the ranch house and the living area on the end for a cook. Then Shermon said, lets add the porch all the way across the front with large beams. Reminton said, so now we have nine bedrooms plus the tenth one is a living area for a live-in cook. There is also a walk-in closet/pantry area and two open fireplaces.

Lance said, man this is going to be a big place. Then they all agreed that it would have to be, plus it would make a perfect ranch house. KaSandra said, it will take some large furniture for these large rooms. They then all agreed that Shermon was right, they would need a large room at times. Cheyenne said, that open staircase is going to be beautiful and big like that large front porch. Reminton said, Shermon told him that anything else would not do.

Chapter 13
They start the Ten-bedroom Ranch House

The next morning Lance said, well Wyatt, are you ready to take that empty wagon to the mill and see if we can fill it? Wyatt said, Lets go!! Reminton told his crew lets lay out this ranch house and dig some holes. Remington said, we need to throw some rock in the bottom of the holes. Then Jesse said, we need to tamp them up right post, really good, before we set those beams. Then we can run the planks that we will use for floor joist from beam to beam. Reminton later said, we have all the post beams and floor joist all set on the mainfloor and it's just about lunch time. We really are doing good.

Then Jesse said, here comes lance and Wyatt with the wood we need. Harry said, that sure is a load of wood but those two oxen look like they are pulling an empty wagon as strong as they are. Lance and Wyatt climbed down from the wagon and was surprised at all the foundation work that was already done. Reminton asked, where's Shorty and Sam. Lance said, they thought they would stay in town and eat at the café today.

Lance said, I told Shorty and Sam seeing how it was Saturday that they could take off until Monday morning. Reminton said, we did put in a couple very long weeks and there has been a lot of talk about big fish in the lake. Lance said, well let's have lunch and then we can unload the wagon and tomorrow is Sunday so whoever wants to catch fish tomorrow for our Sunday meal, I say they should. They had lunch and then they unloaded the wagon and put some long planks over by the three horse shelters. Reminton then said, well I think we did really good, so far so let's knock off until Monday morning. Harry Austin said, I think me, and Mario will go into town and be back Monday morning. Jesse said, I am going to town, also, but I will be back for the fish fry, okay? Reminton said, sure you guys have some fun and then said, Jesse, see you tomorrow afternoon for the fish fry. Then Harry, Mario and Jesse headed towards town.

That evening they were sitting around Autumn's Crossing drinking coffee and getting fishing poles ready for who ever wanted to go fishing on Sunday. KaSandra asked, Reminton, why do you think Harry, Mario and Jesse went to town? Reminton said, Harry and Jesse both had said earlier that they would like to go and have a couple drinks tonight and Shorty and Sam wanted to play some poker at the Tall Branch Saloon, so I guess all four and maybe Mario too will be at the Tall Branch tonight for awhile. KaSandra said, I noticed that they looked like they had a pretty good business so is it just a saloon or is it an eating place too. Reminton said, I haven't been in there, yet, but I met, Duffy Rodman, the owner. Duffy told me that they had a few card tables and served beer and whiskey but if someone wanted a good sit-down meal they needed to go to Potter's Café. That it was a very good place to have a good meal, the coffee was also real good and that Lisa Potter was easy on the eyes. Dakota then asked, you mean she is pretty? Reminton said, I haven't seen her, but I guess she is. Lexi said, I'm sure she is an old lady of thirty years or more and they all laughed.

That evening when they talked of guard duty, Dakota asked, are we always going to have special guard duty? Reminton said, once we get settled in a little more we won't have too. But we are also watching for a mean lion. So, we must be careful of the lion, and until we have doors on our places we will need at least one guard. The next morning Dakota said, it sure looks like a good day to fish. Logon asked, what kind of fish is in our lake? Lance said, Harry told him there was catfish and coal fish. Dakota said, Coal fish? What's a coal fish? Lance said, Harry told him it's a dark color fish and real good eating and even puts up a better fight than a catfish. Wyatt said, I turned over a couple of those logs and found some large worms. Logon said, those are really big worms, so we should catch some really big fish. Reminton said, me and Lance are going to lay out some planks on one of those shelters just to see what it will look like. KaSandra said, it's Sunday and you know we don't work on Sundays. Reminton said, we aren't really going to work.

Wyatt said, do you want me to help you two or go with these guys to the lake? Lance said, Wyatt you go with whoever goes to the lake and watch for that mountain lion. Then Lance said, let's see who all is going to the lake and who is staying here. Dakota, Logon and Lexi, said, they were going to the lake with Wyatt and the rest said they were staying at the building site. Reminton said, well you girls stay on guard at all times. KaSandra said, me and Cheyenne, will have our .44 colts on our sides plus, a rifle with us at all times or anyway close by.

So Reminton and Lance headed over to the first horse shelter and Wyatt headed to the lake with Dakota, Logon and Lexi. They weren't fishing but a short time when they started pulling catfish and coalfish from the lake. Reminton and Lance had the first roof on and decided to start on another one and before they knew it the second roof was done, and they decided to do the third shelter roof. Wyatt said to Dakota, Logon and Lexi, I think we have plenty of fish, what do you guys think? The three said how about we catch one more each then we can clean them. Wyatt said, Okay, just in case we have more people for the fish fry.

They caught three more fish and Wyatt said, lets clean them over at the far end where the water runs out of the lake. They pulled the stringers from the lake and seen they had even more fish than they originally thought they had. Wyatt said, why don't we throw back a few of the smaller ones and we can catch them again when they are bigger. They agreed to it and cleaned twenty-two nice fish for the fish fry. Wyatt was fixing up a fire ring to fry the fish and Logon was bringing over firewood with Dakota and Lexi, when he noticed the large mountain lion down where they were just at cleaning the fish.

Reminton and Lance were on their way back and the lion was between them and the others. Wyatt yelled but they could not shoot because of the cross fire and the lion escaped to the trees. Everyone was looking towards the trees when Jesse Ladrue came riding up and asked what they were looking at. They told him it was the mountain lion, but he was gone now. Jesse said, that lion will be back. Reminton said, when he does come back we will have to make sure we are ready for him. Then Lance said, Jesse we are going to start frying fish. Jesse asked, can I help? Then KaSandra said, you guys relax we will take care of making the meal.

The men sat down with the coffee pot and Jesse said, I noticed the roofs on the three horse shelters. Reminton said, we were going to only do one of the horse shelters but with all the framing done it went so well that before we knew it we had all three horse shelters roofed. Jesse said, well looks like the fishing was good so I guess you could say it was catching, not just fishing. Wyatt said, that's right we kept twenty-two nice large fish and probably threw back ten smaller ones. Lexi asked, what do you mean Jesse, fishing but also catching? Jesse said, it's called fishing because a lot of the time people don't catch fish they just fish for them, or it would be called catching all the time instead of fishing. Lexi said, that makes sense to me, Jesse, with a large smile on her face.

Reminton, Lance and Wyatt drank coffee with Jesse and Reminton asked, Jesse, what would be a good way to leave the main area open and what he thought about the large open staircase for the ranch house? Reminton said, Jesse I don't want to put you in a bad spot, but we know you have done real large projects before. Jesse said, I think you are doing a great job, but I will be happy to help you in any way I can. Lance said, with all the men we have I doThen Ringo rode up and said, he had a telegram from Shermon. Reminton said, well sit down, we will eat real soon, and we have plenty of food. KaSandra said, lets see that telegram. Ringo said, Tim Grant brought it to the marshalls office and the marshall asked me to bring it out to Autumn's Crossing. Lance said, well Ringo did Tim Grant say what was in the telegram? Ringo said, he said that he was okay but him and his cowboys had a little trouble, so he sent this telegram in case any news reached you before he got back. Ringo said, Shermon said, he would tell all when he got back to Autumn's Crossing. Reminton took the telegram and opened it.

The telegram read:

Dear Family,
First, we came on the two wagons one with Gary O'Neal and his wife and three sons'. Mr. O'Neals wife and one son was dead plus, the second wagon was the one that Rick Adams had got from us and Rick Adams was still alive, but in a bad way. Rick Adams later died but first he had given me a leather pouch which he asked me to see that it got to his sister and her family up North and asked me to bury him deep enough to keep the animals away from his body. I have the leather pouch in my saddle bags and I will see that it goes to

Rick Adams sister when I reach Eldorado. The two wagons were attacked by renegade Indians off the reservations. We killed four of them and ran the rest off, but we have been followed by them ever since. Blacky Moore was shot, but only wounded but with Caps help we fixed Blacky up fine. Sundance, Luther and I, are going to pay a visit to the renegade's camp tonight. Luther noticed that a couple of the horses that the renegade rode had shoes on them, unlike Indian ponies. Anyway, closing for now will send another telegram when we reach ElDorado.

Shermon

Reminton said, well let's eat some fish, but first KaSandra would you say a prayer? KaSandra prayed: Lord, thank you for the food we are about to eat and the great fish catching lake here at Autumn's Crossing. Also, Lord, please watch over Shermon and his cowboys and bring them home safe. In God's name we pray, Amen. Oh! P.S. God also keep us safe from that mountain lion. They all then said Amen.

Chapter 14
They Kill the Mountain Lion

Everyone had their fill and Jesse said he wouldn't have to eat tomorrow after eating so much at the fish fry tonight. Jesse blamed it all on the other good food that was put on the table with the fish. Then Reminton said, I heard that lion over in those trees. Ringo said, well unless you want me to go after that lion, I am going to head back to town. Marshall Scott was out of town so Ringo Said, I better get back. Ringo shook hands with the men and thanked the women for the great meal then he thanked Dakota, Logon and Lexi for catching the fish for the fish fry, then headed to town.

Reminton said, well we better get some shut eye as Shermon would say but first I guess we had better clean up this mess and set guard duty for the night. Jesse said, I will stay and have the first watch if you would want me to? Reminton said, well Lance mentioned first watch also, so why not you and Lance on first watch then Wyatt and Logon take the second watch and then Dakota and me will relieve Wyatt and Logon. They all agreed to the watch schedule.

The women all slept with guns and no one got much sleep because the big mountain lion made a lot of noise and was very close at times throughout the night. But the next morning they ate and went about doing what they had planned the night before. Lance and Wyatt headed for the sawmill and Reminton, Jesse, Logon, Harry and Mario worked on the ranch house. When Lance and Wyatt reached the sawmill Shorty Davis met them and asked if they had any trouble with the mountain lion last night? Lance told him that they heard the lion most of the night but that the lion must have moved on well before daylight. Then Shorty said, well I guess that is when the lion must have killed Sam Reitcher after leaving Autumn's Crossing.

Lance and Wyatt both at the same time said, the lion killed Sam? Lance asked, how did it happen? Shorty said, I went by Sams this morning on my way here and only found part of Sam but there was lion tracks and I could see deep cuts on the back of Sam's horse and it looked like Sam was thrown to the ground and I guess that's when the lion got him. Lance said, slow down Shorty so I can follow what you are saying. So, Shorty said, I'm sorry Lance, Sam was my best friend. Lance said, I know but I am trying to figure out how it happened. Shorty said, well it looked like the mountain lion came up behind Sam and his horse and that the lion lunged or sprang for Sam and caught Sams horse and the horse jumped and maybe threw Sam off as he was running away. There was a struggle where Sam hit the ground and I believe that Sam pulled his knife and maybe stabbed the lion at least once. There was a small trail of blood plus Sam's knife was in the trail of blood. Shorty said, and you know the only thing worse than a mountain lion is a wounded mountain lion. Then Deputy, Ringo, rode up and said that he thought the same thing as Shorty that the lion was wounded but maybe not enough to kill the lion.

Then Ringo said, I will let Reminton know what has happened and I'll tell your family to be very careful. Shane rode up and asked if Ringo would mind if he rode with him and Ringo said, he wouldn't mind if Lance and Wyatt were okay with it. Lance and Wyatt both said, they thought it would be a good ideal, also to be, really careful on the way to Autumn's Crossing.

Ringo and Shane rode into Autumn's Crossing and Reminton knew something was wrong before they reached him. Reminton walked over to Ringo and Shane and Harry and Jesse followed a couple of steps behind. Reminton said, what brings you out here Ringo, is something wrong? Ringo said, Sam Reitcher is dead, it looks like the mountain lion got him early this morning. Reminton said, I'm sorry to hear that. That lion was close to us all night but must have left towards Sam's early this morning. Ringo said, theres something else we are sure that Sam stuck the lion at least once with his knife as the lion attacked him and then killed him. We also had to put Sam's horse down the lion really did a number on sam's horse before turning on Sam.

Ringo said, well Reminton I'm heading back to town, but remember now if that lion has been stuck once or more by Sam's knife, he will be even more dangerous than before. Shane then asked Reminton, if it's okay, I will ride back with Ringo to town and then to the sawmill. Reminton said, Shane that is a good ideal, also ask Lance to go over to that pig farm at the edge of town and bring back a small but live pig. When Wyatt and he head back to Autumn's Crossing this evening. Ringo said, Lion bait, right? Reminton said, that's right, Ringo. Then Ringo and Shane headed to town. Reminton then told everyone, at Autumn's Crossing to keep a gun handy, always and to keep their guard up. After that Reminton and his other three carpenters went to work on the main ranch house.

Dakota and Lexi were close by and had caught three or four large rattle snakes but had gotten farther away from the ranch house than they had planned on. Lexi told Dakota, to look at the tall grass, that it looked like there was something large moving through the grass between them and the others. Dakota and Lexi were on foot and they both knew that what they seen moving towards them in the tall grass was the mountain lion. Then they heard the deep throat growling.

As fast as they could they headed towards the other end of the lake and made their way across the water but the only problem other than the mountain lion was that they were heading away from everyone else and now they knew they were on their own and that the mountain lion was stalking them.

Back at the site of the new ranch house to be, Reminton and his carpenters as they were called were already washed up for supper and were looking at the work that they had done that day. Lance and Wyatt were pulling up with a wagon load of lumber and a squealing unhappy pig when they heard KaSandra and Brandy calling for Dakota and Lexi. Then Cheyenne came over and said they had seen Dakota and Lexi catching rattle snakes but now they were not for sure where they were, but they did hear the lion down by the lake.

Lance and Wyatt jumped down from the wagon. Lance said, we need to spread out and find Dakota and Lexi and kill that lion. Jesse, Harry and Mario asked, what are we waiting for let's go get that lion. Reminton said, take that pig down to the lake and let him squeal. Stay close together and let's hope that lion comes for the pig then we will kill it. Then Reminton said, KaSandra you and Cheyenne check your guns and see that Abigail and Brandy has a rifle or a shot gun if they prefer.

Reminton said, I hate to leave but I'm sure that Dakota and Lexi went towards the lake. Now I'm also sure that the lion is between us and them. Jesse said, Reminton it will be getting dark real soon. Reminton said, yea we might have an hour before it's dark. KaSandra asked do you want me and Cheyenne to go with you? Reminton said, stay with Valerie and Katelyn, and be really careful, that cat is smart, and he might double back, when he knows we are stalking him. So Reminton, Lance, Wyatt and Jesse headed towards the lake. Reminton said, make some noise so that lion will hear us coming.

Dakota and Lexi had made it to a small cave and were inside. Then Lexi seen all the bones and yelled "this is the lion's den!" Dakota said, start gathering all the sticks you can find and throw them in that opening. Dakota said, I will put these couple larger logs with them plus we need to throw as many leaves on the pile as we can. Then Dakota said, lets throw these four rattle snakes in with the sticks. The snakes were making a lot of noise. Dakota said, the more noise these snakes make the better. Dakota asked Lexi to poke the pile of sticks, so the snakes would keep rattleing. Then Dakota said, I will tie my knife on the end of this strong stick.

Lexi said, the mountain lion is here you can hear his deep throat growling and I can even see his large white teeth. Dakota told Lexi it's just a matter of time before that lion either comes through them snakes or finds another way in. It was dark in the cave and Dakota told Lexi to get behind him and he would kill the lion with his knife if the lion came through the snakes. Dakota was worried as Lexi was, but he would try and save her no matter what happened.

Then, all the sudden, there was a big light in the sky, then a roll of thunder, then the rain was coming down. At first it was light rain then it was raining very hard. Dakota said, thank you God and told Lexi we will be okay now, I think. They waited about five more minutes then Dakota moved the snakes out of the way and put them back in the cave and said, we will get these another day. With most of the sticks out of the way Dakota told Lexi follow me and stay as close as you can and keep running. Lexi asked, what about the mountain lion? Dakota said, that cat will not stay in the rain, but if it quits, he will be after us again. So, come on, lets run as fast as we can.

Back at the ranch when the hard rain started Harry told Mario and Logon to come under the horse shelter with him. Then Mario said, I see Reminton and the other three men heading back. Logon asked do you see Dakota and Lexi? Dakota and Lexi are no where in sight, said Mario. KaSandra said, when that last lightening flash lit up the sky I seen the four men heading back, but I did not see Dakota or Lexi. When Reminton stepped up on the back porch he said, well I hope those two kids are safe and holed up somewhere dry. Dakota is smart and so is Lexi from what I've seen of her. KaSandra said, we need to go find them now. Reminton said, we will head out again at first light. We need to pray that Dakota got him and Lexi somewhere safe and that the lion did not catch them in the open. As long as, it keeps raining like this that lion will hole up somewhere dry. Then Reminton said, but if it stops or when it stops we need to be ready. The lion will be on there trail again or back here.

Reminton said, we might as well put some more coffee on because I believe it will be a long night. Harry, Mario and Logon had a nice fire going under the horse shelter, but Harry said, I sure wish we had some coffee. Logon took off towards the place that Shermon once called a shack. Harry yelled, where are you going Logon? Logon said, I will be right back. It wasn't no time and Logon was back. Logon said I brought a small coffee pot full of coffee. Harry said, thanks, but we need to stay close to this fire.

Brandy and Wyatt were praying that Dakota and Lexi were okay. Then the rest also joined in with prayers, as they all said in gods name, amen there was a large flash of lightening and the rain had almost stopped. Then there were three gunshots and yelling outside. Harry had fired the three shots into the air when him and Mario seen Dakota and Lexi making there way across the lake. Reminton was the first one to the door with everyone right behing him with their guns.

As they all ran out the back door, Reminton said, there's Dakota and Lexi. Look Harry and Mario are running towards the lake with a couple of torches. Reminton and Wyatt then started running towards the lake. Dakota said, don't look back, keep running Lexi! Everyone was yelling to Dakota and Lexi. Reminton said, that lion is going to cross that lake soon. They seen Lexi fall and Dakota stopped to help Lexi up and told her keep running! Wyatt yelled to Dakota, "run son the lion is close to crossing the lake!" Reminton yelled, he just crossed the water! Reminton, Wyatt, Harry and Mario met Dakota and Lexi at the same time. Dakota and Lexi kept running towards Lance and the women and Dakota said, don't stop running Lexi! As Dakota and Lexi made the porch the guns were going off, but Dakota and Lexi went in the back door and fell on the floor. Reminton, Wyatt, Harry and Mario must have put ten to twelve bullets in the lion when Reminton said, I think he's dead, what do you think, Harry? Harry said, I'm sure he is, and he better be because that was to close this time.

They drug the lion to the shack. Dakota and Lexi looked at the mountain lion and then at each other. Dakota said, Lexi, I am glad that you are okay, and Lexi said, I am because of you Dakota. Harry said to Mario, lets skin this big mountain lion and Mario agreed to it. Then all the questions came. Where were you two? How come you two were so far out? And on and on with the questions from everyone. Wyatt came in and hugged Dakota and Lexi, and said Son, I am sure glad you and Lexi made it back and we would like to know what happened out there, if you two feel up to talking about it now.

Dakota said, well we were wrangling snakes and got towards the lake when we noticed that the lion had got between us and the shack. Lexi said, I noticed the lion first but then I didn't know what to do, but Dakota saved us. Brandy hugged Dakota and Lexi, and then asked what did you two do that saved you from that lion? Dakota said, well that lion was stalking us for sure, we knew that. So, we headed across the stream at the far side of the lake and up to where there was a shallow cave with a small opening. We filled the opening with sticks and rock as many as we could find. There was plenty of wood to block the opening, but I knew that alone would not stop the lion, so I put the four large rattle snakes in the limbs and teased them, so they would rattle. KaSandra said, that was a very good ideal. Dakota said, I tied my skinning knife on a strong limb because that was the only weapon we had, and I told Lexi to stay behind me. Lexi said, Dakota said, if that mountain lion gets me he wanted me to run for all I was worth and not stop until I got back here. But I wasn't going to leave him to fight that lion alone. I also had my dad's knife out and ready. Reminton said Dakota, is that why you left your boots because you used your shoe strings to tie your knife on the stick?

Dakota said, I still had my boots on when we ran from the cave but when we hit the water, the water was up and running pretty strong, so I lost my boots in the water. Lexi said, and if that old piece of fence wasn't at the end of the lake I don't think we could have made it across the water. Cheyenne said, well I'm sure glad that the old fence was there and you two got across the water, then Cheyenne hugged Dakota and Lexi. Brandy asked, why did you two leave the safety of the cave? It was only time before that mountain lion would have came through the mouth of that cave, so that hard rain and lightening flashes was God sent. Lexi said, that hard rain drove the lion into cover and after a few minutes, Dakota said, it was time to make our escape and he told me to stay close and don't stop running no mater what. Then when the rain stopped we both knew the lion would be on our trail again.

Then Harry and Mario came in with the largest hide that anyone of them had ever seen. Mario said, who wants this hide? Dakota said, can we have it after it hangs awhile? Everyone agreed that Dakota and Lexi should have the hide, so they stretched it out under the overhang at the back side of the so-called shack and it covered a very large area of the back wall. Jesse came in and said, well what should we do with this pig now that we don't need it anymore? Reminton said, well I guess we could either take it back to the pig farm, or we could keep him and eat it later. Then Valerie and Katelyn both said, Lets keep "Charlie", but we don't want to eat him, just keep him as a pet. Lance said, you already gave him a name, so I don't see how we can eat a pig with a name. Then Jesse said, it would be easy to keep plus if given a chance the pig would eat snakes and even mice.

Chapter 15
They keep " Charlie", and get another pig to smoke

Dakota said, its okay to keep the pig and name him Charlie, but Charlie had better not eat any of my snakes. Katelyn and Valerie both said, you keep your snakes away from Charlie and he won't eat them. Dakota and Lexi both agreed to it. Reminton said, tomorrow is Sunday so whoever wants to go to town tomorrow with me can. I want to check at the telegram office to see if there is a telegram from Shermon, plus get another pig to smoke. KaSandra said, but we don't have a smoker. Then Reminton said, we will have, Jesse is going to build one tomorrow with Harry's help.

Lance said, I think I could sleep now, but I guess we need to set up guard duty first. Reminton said, I will take first watch, if someone wants to relieve me in a couple of hours and then Wyatt said, he would take second and Lance said, he would relieve Wyatt. Jesse said, he was going into town and he would be back in the morning and start on the smoker. Shane said, that he would ride in with Jesse.

So, after a little sleep they all felt better in the morning. After finishing breakfast, Jesse and Shane rode back towards Autumn's Crossing. They had a heavy iron box for the smoker and other pieces that they were going to use for making the fire box for the smoker. Jesse asked Reminton if he could use some lumber that was brought back from the saw mill. Reminton said, for Jesse to use whatever lumber he needed. Harry said he would help Jesse build the smoker and that Shane said he would take Mario and Logon to cut some oak, hickory and some mesquite for the smoking.

So Reminton, KaSandra, Lance, Abigail, Dakota and Lexi headed to town. First, they stopped by the telegraph office and sure enough, Tim Gates had a telegram from Shermon. Tim Gates, the owner of the telegraph office, said Shermon had some trouble but he was on his way back to Autumn's Crossing. Reminton said, thanks Tim, but we will read it!

After leaving the telegraph office they sat down and read the telegram.

Shermon said, we had some renegade Indian trouble but not to bad, plus some weather problems but we got through it okay. Will be bringing some beef cattle and hopefully a few mustangs back with us. Closing for now. See you all in a couple weeks.

Shermon

Reminton said, that means Shermon should be back in less than two weeks. Because this wire is four days old. So maybe ten or twelve days. Shermon will be back. So, lets do what we must in town and head back to Autumn's Crossing. The six of them headed out to the pig farm and talked with the owners, Brett and Maria Clay, and asked if they needed to do anything special for Charlie, the pig that the girls wanted to keep. Brett told them that Charlie would not squeal so much and maybe hardly at all if he had some company. Lance said, you mean another pig? Brett said, that's right and that two pigs were even less trouble than one. KaSandra said, that she did not think they would want a bunch of baby pigs. Brett and Maria both said, that Charlie was really a girl and if they got another sow or girl pig they would not have to worry about baby pigs, plus later they would still have lots of bacon if they wanted to smoke one or both pigs. So, they said they would take another small pig with about the same markings of Charlie, but enough to tell them apart. Also, they would like a larger pig butchered for them to smoke now and asked if Brett could deliver them to Autumn's Crossing. Brett said, he would deliver both later that day.

So, the six then headed to the general store. Micka and Daniel were very happy to see the six people from Autumn's Crossing. Daniel asked, what they were needing today. KaSandra said, that they had a list, but they did not bring a wagon with them. Micka said, well if you would like to leave the list, I will bring it all out later today. Reminton said, there is a couple things we will want to take with us, then you can bring the rest. When they agreed to that, they called Dakota over to where the boots were and said to Dakota, lets see if they have your size. Dakota said, I have these old boots and I like them. KaSandra said, you can keep those old boots, but we talked and decided that maybe you could use a new pair also. Dakota said, well I like those two-tone ones that zip up the side, but I don't know if they have my size. Micka then said, let me see what size you need we have larger size boots in that style. Then Micka said, Dakota you need a size twelve and I know we have that size in the back store room and headed back to get them.

Lexi was looking at a pair of cowgirl boots when KaSandra walked over to her. KaSandra said, Lexi, if you like them boots let's get them. Lexi said, I don't think I want to spend that much of my money, but I do like them. KaSandra said, Lets see what size you need the ranch will buy them. Lexi said, I can wait until I can afford them. Then Reminton said, you can get them now. Dakota and you are both getting new boots. For bringing that mountain lion to us where we could kill it. Lexi said, well okay, as long as I earned it, I will take the boots and Thank you very much. Dakota and Lexi both wore their new boots as they walked out of the general store. They all had a few items that they took with them and then decided to have the rest delivered that evening by Micka.

When they got back to Autumn's Crossing there was a large smoker ready for smoking plus a good size pig pen. KaSandra said, I'm glad you made that pig pen as big as you did. Jesse asked, Why? KaSandra said well we figured that Charlie might need a friend, so we got another pig. Katelyn and Valerie both squealed and said you mean now we have two pet pigs. Reminton said, that's right. Lance said, it looks like Shermon will be back in ten or twelve days. Jesse and Harry both said, well I hope he is happy with the work we have done so far. Reminton said, I know he will be, but we still have a few days to get a roof on this ranch house before he gets back.

Abigail came out and said, we have some food ready for anyone that might be hungry. The guys walked over to the pump handle and washed up, then sat down at the large table. There was eight men sitting at the table, then Dakota, Lexi and even blue tried to get to the table. Then Valerie got ahold of blue and said for him to come with her to meet Charlie. They had a great supper and plenty of black coffee. The men were sittng around the table talking of their plans for the next few days. Reminton said, that it would take all of them to put the roof on the ranch house. Lance said, how about me and Wyatt going to the sawmill in the morning and come back at lunch time? Reminton said, that would be great. By the time Lance, Wyatt and Shorty got to Autumn's Crossing for lunch he thought that he and his so called carpenters would be ready to put the roof on after lunch.

Then Brett and Maria Clay pulled up at Autumn's Crossing in a small wagon with two crates in the back of the wagon. One was the other small pig to keep Charlie company, which Valerie and Katelyn hurried away with. They were already calling the other little pig buster. Maria Clay said to Brett, the girls name one female pig Charlie, so I guess they should name the other little girl pig, Buster and laughed. The other covered crate had a large butchered pig in it ready for the smoker. Jesse and Harry already had the fire box full of oak and hickory to smoke the pig. Jesse showed KaSandra, Abigail and Brandy plus the others how to put the meat on the racks and how the smoker worked. Jesse said, by morning that meat will be so tender and ready to eat whenever you want, plus there is a lot of bacon for the days to come. They all thanked Jesse and Harry for the great smoker that they would be able to use for many years to come.

Reminton said, here comes Micka and Daniel with our supplies. When they pulled into Autumn's Crossing KaSandra asked them did you close the general store early? Daniel said no, I wanted to ride out here with Micka, so we have Hank Patterson watching the store while we are gone. Hank works for us and normally makes the deliveries, but we decided to make this one ourselves. KaSandra and Abigail both said, they were glad they did. KaSandra said, let me show you around a little. Daniel said, first I need to help Micka unload your supplies. KaSandra said we have people here who will unload that wagon.

Micka, Daniel, plus Brett and Maria were all very impressed with what they seen at Autumn's Crossing. They also seen the very large mountain lion hide and said, how lucky Dakota and Lexi had been when they heard the story of how Dakota and Lexi escaped the lion. Then after some coffee and biscuits with honey, the Grants and the Clay's both said they needed to head back. After hugs and handshakes, the Grant's and the Clay's headed back to town.

So Reminton said, well as Shermon would say whoever is staying let's set guard duty and the rest get some shut eye. Jesse said, me, Harry and Shane are going into town, so we will see you all in the morning. Mario said, he was also going to town and Shorty said, he would be at the sawmill in the morning. Reminton said, Well, Shorty, if you want to clean up and stack those short pieces at the sawmill go ahead and then come to Autumn's Crossing at lunch time. After lunch we will need everyone we can get on this ranch house roof.

Four days later they had the entire roof on and all the walls layed out inside for all the interior walls. They had two large fireplace boxes in the great room with stacks cut through the roof. They had openings cut out in every room and small glass panes inserted in the openings with a door leading into the greatroom from every bedroom, plus a large heavy double door leading out of the great room onto a very large covered porch with a hitching post across the front of the covered porch and on a large support post to the left side of the steps was a very large bell which was engraved with the words Kansas City, MO and on the other side of the of the steps was a large black dinner bell. If the dinner bell was rigning it was time to eat, but if the large Kansas City, MO bell was ringing there was possible trouble.

Reminton said, well Shermon will be back anyday now so we will start on the bunk house next, I guess? Wyatt asked, what about this place here that started out as a shack? Reminton said, I think it will make good storage as we build the other buildings.

Chapter 16
Shermon and his Cowboys pull into Autumn's Crossing

The next couple of days they finished the large ranch house and Reminton told the women to move their things into the rooms. Reminton said, lets stretch a fence at the low end of the lake and build a nice platform out into the lake. They left the end room for Shermon, and KaSandra, Abigail, and Brandy all took a room, then Cheyenne said, if it's okay? I will throw my things in this room downstairs for now. So, KaSandra told the kids to take a room and Dakota, Logon, Lexi all took a room and Valerie and Katelyn wanted to share a room. KaSandra said, well that's all nine bedrooms plus the large live in cook's room/bedroom. Cheyenne said, there will be an extra one, when I move in with Shermon, but first we have to be married. KaSandra said, I can hardly wait for that day. Cheyenne said, When Shermon is ready we will get married. Cheyenne then said, I really like how the four large bedrooms are upstairs and how the open stairway is all the way across the front of the four bedrooms. Brandy said, plus how the five other bedrooms open into the large open area was the best way to go. Abigail said, there was also a lot of thought that went into the cook's room on the outside of the kitchen.

Reminton had the twelve quarterhorses in the corral on one end there was a dividing gate that had an area they could fence off separate with one horse shelter. The rest of the large corral was one large area with two horse shelters. On the back side of the corral was a small area for the two pigs if needed. Reminton was not sure what Shermon would think of two pigs running loose on their horse ranch. Reminton asked the other eight men all to work on the bunkhouse with him. Reminton said, there will be eight bunks across the back wall with foot lockers. We will also have storage under the beds. There will be a door out the back plus a door out the front. On the front there will be four more bunks with foot lockers and more storage under those bunks. Reminton said, as you can see on this drawing there will be a large fire place open to both sides with a table and chairs on either side of the fireplace. We will build a covered porch across the whole front. As Reminton was showing the drawings, Harry yelled, here come the horses and the cows and KaSandra was ringing the Kansas City bell. Jesse said, looks like they have a lot of cows.

Shermon yelled, open the gate! Reminton said, look at that black stallion that Shermon has tied behind Buck. KaSandra said, looks like they have atleast fifty cows, plus the wild horses. Lexi said, look at those two young horses! Shermon yelled to Luther Green and Wes Montana, put the two young colts in with our twelve quarter horses in the small corral. Shermon yelled, Kid, put the stallion and nine mustangs in the large corral, plus the sixty-five head of cattle for now. Shermon said, I want to leave this lead rope on this black stallion for a little while.

After the nine mustang mares settled down and the stallion calmed down Shermon took off the lead rope and the mustangs and stallion stood under the one shelter. Shermon said, lets just let the cattle stand where they want, as long as that stallion stays with them mustangs. Luther, Nevada and Shane took pitchforks and forked a little hay and took the covers off the three water troughs. Shermon said, looks like this is going pretty well, keep an eye on that stallion. Shermon said, I can see everyone has been busy hear at Autumn's Crossing.

Shermon Shook hands with his three brothers plus with Jesse and Harry. Shermon hugged his brothers' wives. Cheyenne was standing on the large porch. Shermon smiled at Cheyenne. Cheyenne smiled at Shermon and stepped off the porch. In two or three steps Shermon had Cheyenne in his arms and they kissed what seemed like forever. Cheyenne said, did you miss me big man? Shermon said, I sure did, and I could not help worrying about that mountain lion.Lexi said we got that lion Sherm. Dakota, Logon and Mario said glad you are back and shook hands with Shermon. Valerie and Katelyn ran up and hugged Shermon. Then Lexi came up and hugged Shermon and said again, we got that lion Sherm. Shermon said, I want to hear about that after I knock off some of this dust. I know you want to hear about our trail drive and I want to hear what all happened while I was gone. Shermon asked Reminton to get the strong box so he could pay his cowboys and the carpenters.

Shermon said, I know there is a lot to talk about and there is a lot for me to see. But first I would like to get a biscuit for me and my cowboys and for anyone else that would like to eat. Then after we eat, Reminton, we need to pay our cowboys and carpenters for the great job they have done in one month's time. KaSandra said, we have smoked pork and it won't take no time to have all the side's ready. Shermon said, we will knock off some of this dust and be right back. When they walked back KaSandra said, the coffee is hot. Shermon said, look at this meal. I noticed the large smoker and it looks like it works as good as it looks. Cheyenne said, it does, eat up big man. We have the smoked pork, biscuits, some side items and there are two large blackberry pies.

After they ate all they could Shermon asked Reminton to get the strong box from the safe and the pay ledger. When they came to Sam Reitcher's name Reminton told Shermon that the lion killed him, and his horse had to be shot. Shermon asked Shorty Davis if Sam had any family and Shorty said no. But there is a girl in town that he liked a lot. Shermon Said, give her Sam's pay and tell her how sorry we are, and that Sam was a good man. Shorty said, I gave the undertake Shorty's saddle and rifle, but he told me to keep his Colt 44.

Shermon asked Reminton to put up the strong box and for him and the nine other men to meet him at the bunkhouse. Then Shermon said, there is 8 bunks on the back wall and 4 bunks on the front wall. They all have a footlocker and a storage under the bunk. Shermon said, Kid you and Harry pick your bunks. Harry took the front one on the right side of the door. Mario took the one next to the one Harry took. Wes took the one on the left side of the door on the front wall and Jesse took the one next to him. Sundance, Luther, Blackie, Nevada and Shane all threw their bed rolls on a bunk on the back wall. Shermon said that leaves three open bunks.

Wes Montana said, that really looks good how that fireplace is open on both sides. Harry said and there is plenty of room for everyone at those two tables. Jesse said, that covered porch will be great to drink coffee or just enjoy. Luther said, there sure is plenty of room in this bunkhouse. Shermon was saying how this bunkhouse has a large footlocker from floor to ceiling for each bunk plus the under storage under the bunks. Shermon said, once the blacksmith shop is built there will be a horse stall for every cowboy. There will also be a storage locker in each horse stall plus a place to hang your horses saddle.

Reminton walked in and asked, well what's everyone think about this bunkhouse? All the cowboys agreed it was better than they hoped for. Shermon said, Reminton everyone that worked on this bunkhouse did a real good job. Then Shermon said, I told the men about their own horse stall and storage locker that will be in the blacksmith shop when it's built. But Reminton, this porch I think we should make it the full length of the bunk house. Also, a roof over the whole porch with a couple of tables and chairs and do away with the benches. That's sounds good, Reminton Said, anything else, big brother? Shermon said, yea we need two hitching posts and a long watering trough at the hitching rails. Shermon said, Reminton believe me I love what you all have done. But I want our cowboys to be as happy as we can make them. Reminton said, I want them to be as happy as possible also Sherm.

Then Shermon said, I will see you nine cowboys in the morning. I am going to spend a little time with my family. Reminton said, I am glad that it is so early Shermon, because not only do we have a lot to tell you we also want to hear about your trail drive, plus all the money that you gave me to put in the safe. They started to walk out when Cap told Shermon, if it's okay I will just grab one of the three extra bunks for tonight and we will talk about me moving in the bedroom off the kitchen or sleeping here later. Shermon said, if that's what you want, it's okay with me. See you in the morning Cap.

Then Shermon looked at the large ranch home and said this is even more than I hoped for. Shermon said, you all have got so much more done than I would have ever dreamed of. Reminton said, Sherm, everyone pulled together and it wasn't bad at all. Shermon said, that is the most important thing, if we keep the men happy there is nothing that they wouldn't do to make us happy. Shermon then said, I want to thank you all for everything that you did while I was on the trail.

Shermon said, I have a couple ideals to add to the great things that you all have done. But we can talk about that later. First, I would like to hear about that mountain lion, I seen his hide hanging out back, I like it there. Reminton said, I think it's only right that Dakota and Lexi tell you because it is because of them that we got the lion. Shermon said, okay, Dakota and Lexi, tell me what happened. Dakota said, me and Lexi was wrangling snakes when the lion got between us and everyone else. So, we took off across the lake and we got into a shallow cave. We filled the opening with sticks and rocks and then I threw the four large rattle snakes in the opening and teased them, so they would rattle. The lion heard the snakes and they kept him from coming right in on us. I knew it was only a matter of time before the lion did get in, so I tied my skinning knife, the one you gave me, on a good stick with my boot strings. Thank God it started raining really hard and the lion headed for cover. Because after a couple of minutes of real hard rain, me and Lexi headed back here as fast as we could run. I lost my boots in the water, but we kept running and didn't stop until we made it back.

Reminton said, we seen Dakota and Lexi running as the lightening was flashing. But then we seen the lion making his way at the edge of the lake and he was on Dakota and Lexi's back trail. Lexi slipped and fell once but she did not stop she was back up running as fast as she could. Lexi said, Dakota kept me going even when I thought I couldn't go anymore. Reminton said, as Dakota and Lexi ran buy us Dakota was yelling shoot, shoot, but he kept on running towards Lance and the rest. Dakota said, as we made it to the porch, we heard the shooting.

Reminton said, we put maybe ten bullets in that lion before we brought him down. Lexi said, Sherm I was so afraid, and Dakota told me to stay behind him and he was holding the knife you gave him, and I had my dads knife in my hand. Dakota said, if the lion came in he would kill him and for me to run for help. Lexi said, I was praying that somehow, we would live. Shermon said, well I'll be. You two did really good, and I am glad the lion is dead.

Reminton said, the lion killed Sam and stalked others, but he hung around too long.

Shermon said, yea it sounds like that lion was pretty smart, but he messed up when he came to Autumn's Crossing. Shermon said, well I am glad that it is over and glad that he is hanging on our back wall. But more than that I am glad no one here got hurt. Shermon said, I am glad to be home, but I will be leaving again in about two weeks. There is a lot of cows out there for the taking and more horses for our horse ranch. The mustangs are running wild and the cattle is waiting to be picked up. I was told in Eldorado that they would buy all the beef they could get, plus they would be interested in some good horses from us.

Reminton will you get that strong box from the safe so everyone can see why I must go back? Plus, I will tell you what Rick Adams made me promise him and I did tell him I would. Also, we had a little other trouble on the trail that I will tell you about. There is a little danger out on the trail, but that is why no one else is on the trail. I can see us building a great horse ranch and selling some beef.

Chapter 17
Shermon tells of the Cattle drive
and his future plans

Shermon said, we weren't out two days when we heard the shooting and headed to it. Rick Adams and Gary O'Neal's two wagons were being attacked by renegade Indians. We rode in with guns a blazing and we killed four of the renegades, but we figured at least eight made it to the trees. Rick Adams was in a real bad way and Gary O'Neals wife and one son had been killed. So, we buried O'Neal's wife and one son. Then we did what we could for Rick Adams and then buried Rick after he died. But before Rick died he gave me a money pouch with Nine Thousand, Five Hundred dollars in it in cash plus a deed to a place of property.

Rick said if I promised to get the money to his sister up north and build a one room school house and name it Carloline Adams, School house. If I would build it on the piece of property that was close to the mill, he would sign the dead of the saw mill over to me in which he did. Rick also marked the Three thousand dollar note paid in full. I told Rick that I would get the money to his sister and build the school house plus add the name of his wife to the front over the door. I told Rick he did not have to sign over the mill I would do what he asked and still pay the Three Thousand dollars. But Rick signed the note over to me anyway and would not take the money.

After we buried the three and marked there graves we said a few words over them. Gary O'Neal signed as witness to the sawmill deed and what else took place. Then O'Neal took his two son's and said they would hook up with a large wagon train later. Gary O'Neal said, it was leaving in a couple weeks and now he knew he should have waited. Shermon said, I was sorry, but there was no way of knowing what was going to happen. So, they left to hookup with the wagon train and we hooked back up with our cows that we had.

We were picking up quite a few head of cattle and we seen others. We also seen a couple of other stallions and we seen quite a few mustang mares and young colts. There was some young stallions or colts that had been driven off and now they had become a bachelor band of young stallions. We were bedding down for the night when Luther came in and said, there was a large beautiful black stallion with nine or ten mares close in a small canyon. Also, he had seen maybe twenty or more head of beef in the next valley. So, we decided to stay clear of them until we started back and catch them in the canyon on our way back to Autumn's Crossing.

Two days later we noticed that we were still being tailed. So that night Cap and Luther stayed with our herd. Then me, Kid, Sundance, Blacky and Nevada decided to pay our not so sneaky trailers an unexpected visit in their camp. We rode right in to their camp and believe me the renagades were suprised. There was nine dead renagades killed that night. And as far as they believe their spirit will never find them in the dark. The Indian believes they will wonder in the dark forever if killed at night. Anyway, it looked like we had missed three or four because of the tracks. Wes pointed out that one of the riders must have been very heavy because of the deep tracks left by his horse and also his horse had shoes on. We headed back to our camp and after a couple hours of sleep and a fast biscuit in the morning we were back on the trail. We were not being followed anymore and we made good time.

We reached Eldorado with five hundred thirty beef that we sold for Thirty-two dollars, a head. Then we sold the wagon and two oxen that Rick Adams gave back to us. We got an even Thousand dollars for it. Which now totals Seventeen thousand nine hundred sixty dollars. Reminton that is what should be in that pouch I gave you, plus the Three thousand dollar note for the saw mill. If you will count it and then note it in our ledger as Twenty thousand, nine hundred sixty dollars total. Rem, if you will see what our total is after paying our cowboys and carpenters, plus what you have deducted for the general store and any other cost we have acquired and let me know the total when you get it.

Shermon got himself a cup of coffee and walked out on the porch. Cheyenne came out and kissed Shermon and Shermon hugged her. Shermon asked, are you going to be okay with this? Cheyenne said, I will stand by your side. There was candle oil light coming from the bunkhouse a little smoke drifting up from the stove pipe and guitar music with singing.

Reminton called to Shermon, I have the talley. Reminton said, with the Fifteen thousand four hundred sixty dollars we had in the cash box after paying all debts then the Sixteen thousand, nine hundred sixty dollars we received for the five hundred thirty head of beef cattle and the one thousand for the wagon and two oxen that you sold in Eldorado we have a grand total of Thirty-three thousand, four hundred twenty dollars plus the Three thousand dollars we kept at Rick Adams request. Shermon said that is really good, Thirty-six thousand, four hundred and twenty dollars.

Then Shermon handed Reminton the nine thousand, five hundred, which Rick Adams had intrusted in him and asked him to put it plus the deed to the piece of land on which the one room school house was to be built on, also in the strong box in a separate place. Next, Shermon handed Reminton the last deed which was the deed to the Sawmill with Rick Adams signing the deed over to Shermon and also had Gary O'Neal's name as witness on the deed. Shermon said, tomorrow we will take the Nine thousand, five hundred dollars to Arthur Travis, the president of the Waco bank and ask Mr. Travis to wire the money to Rick Adams sister, also we will talk about us building a one room school house in the name of Caroline Adams, on the piece of property at the edge of town.

Now there is something else, Shermon said, I would like to buy a large piece of land adjoining our land. There is three thousand two hundred acres with no water rights and we can get it for Three thousand two hundred dollars, which is only One dollar an acre. The real good thing is once we add the three thousand two hundred acres to our Six thousand four hundred acres it will have water rights, so the new value will be Ten dollars an acre or Thirty-two thousand dollars. That would make our land Nine thousand six hundred acres. Fifteen miles long by Ten miles wide.

It would take one full day to ride from point A to point B. From ranch to other end of our land. Now is the time to buy, we can put the beef across the lake on part of the new land and keep most of the horses on the ranch, leaving more room than needed. Shermon was still tryin to sell his family on the second piece of property when Reminton said, save your breath Shermon, we also were hoping to convince you on the other land. That's good Sheron said, so in the morning we will go see Arthur Travis at the bank. Then Shermon said, I am ready for some shut eye how abou the rest of you. That night was the first night that they all slept under one roof in a long time. The next morning, they woke up to the dinner bell being hit by Cap. They had a good breakfast then Shermon asked, three of the men to go to the mill and start cutting wood for the one room school house.

Wyatt took Shane Madison, Shorty Davis and Logon with him to the sawmill. Then Shermon asked Lance to take Jesse Ladrue, Harry Austin and Harry's son Mario to the piece of property at the edge of town where the school house was going to be built and lay out the building, after they got what they needed at the sawmill for the foundation. Reminton, I would like for you to come to town with me with the money to be wired to Rick Adams sister, plus the deed to the property where the school will be built and we will go see Arthur Travis at the bank and after that is done we will see if we can give Mr. Travis the money for the land joining ours.

Then Shermon pulled out the branding iron that he had showed to his family last night for their approval and then handed it to Wes Montana and said, Kid you take Sundance Ried, Blacky Moore, Nevada Smith and Luther Green with you. Have someone start a good fire and get that branding iron hot while the rest of you stretch two strands of wire large enough to hold twenty to twenty-five head of beef then brand those cattle with this branding iron. Wes Montana looked at the branding iron it was an A/C, A slash C for Autumn's Crossing. Shermon also said, Kid if you get a chance move those pigs to an area farther away from where we eat and sleep. They all laughed and Shermon and Reminton rode towards town.

They pulled up to the bank and Arthur Travis walked out and shook their hands and asked, what brings you to town today? Shermon explained the Nine thousand Five hundred dollars and about the one room school house and mentioned the Thirty-two hundred acres adjoining Autumn's Crossing. Arthur said, lets take care of the Nine thousand, five hundred dollars first and wire the money to Rick Adams sister with a note from Shermon explaining what had taken place and then he said How sorry they all were about the death of her brother. While the banker, Arthur Travis and Shermon were talking about the thirty-two hundred acres the owner of the property sent a wire to the bank.

To the President of Waco Texas Bank; Mr. Arthur Travis: The Price of the thirty-two hundred acres is one dollar an acre, but two thousand, five hundred dollars, if all thirty-two hundred is sold at once.

Arthur Travis showed the telegram to Shermon and Reminton. Shermon said, Rem, count out, two thousand, five hundred dollars, and then asked Arthur Travis if he had a bill of sale for the property. Arthur said, I sure do, and it is already signed by the owner and all it needs is for me to sign it. Well then, sign it Mr. Travis, and we will give you the two thousand, five hundred dollars for the deed and a signed receipt. Mr. Travis handed Shermon the deed and a signed receipt which Shermon looked at and then handed it to Reminton and shook Arthur Travis' hand. Then while Reminton was shaking the Bank presidents hand the banker said Shermon I have another wire here from Rick Adams sister.

Dawn Marie Adams said, in her wire:

Dear Mr. Shermon McBay:

Thank you for everything that you did for me and my brother. About the one room school house being named Caroline Adams, I think it's great. Also, I teach home shooling at my house now and if there is a need for a school mom at the Caroline School I would be very interested. Will be waiting to hear from you.

Yours truly,

Dawn Marie Adams.

Shermon said, well we have a school mom, so we had better get a school built. Shermon and Reminton stopped by the telegraph office and had Tim Gates send a wire to Dawn Marie Adams.

Miss Dawn Marie,

We will be looking for you. Let us know when you will arrive. The one room school house will be ready.

Yours truly,

Shermon McBay.

Then they stopped by the sawmill and Lance was there. Lance, Wyatt, Shorty and Logon were loading the last of the lumber on a wagon to take to the site where the school house was going to be built. Shermon told them of Dawn Marie Adams and that she would be on her way to Waco in about two weeks. Shermon said, that she was Rick Adams sister and she was going to be the school mom.

Shermon, Reminton, Lance, Wyatt, Shorty and Logon all rode over to the site at the edge of town where the school was to be built. The foundation was completed and looked good. Shermon said, well let's leave this wagon of lumber here and you guys can get a start on it in the morning. Shorty said, he was going to stay in town and that he would be with the wagon. So, the five mcBays headed back to Autumn's Crossing to see how things were going back at the ranch. When they got back to Autumn's Crossing Shermon asked Reminton to take a tally on the strong box and they would discuss it later this evening.

Then Shermon rode down to where Wes Montana was. Shermon said, Kid the two wire fence looks good and I'm sure it will hold whatever beef we put in there. So how is the branding going, Shermon then asked? Wes Montana said, we have 25 head branded and we have 5 more that we will brand in the next hour. Shermon said, that's real good kid.

Wes asked, how did it go in town? Real good, Shermon said, plus we have a school mom as soon as the one room school is ready. Wes asked, do I know her? Shermon said, it is Rick Adams sister, Dawn Marie. Wes said, you must be kidding me. No, I'm not kidding you, is there something wrong with her Kid, asked Shermon? Wes Montana said, no, does Nevada know that Dawn Marie is coming back to Waco? Shermon said, you are the only one that I have told. Does Nevada like her? Wes said, Like her? He was in love with her, but she was not ready to settle down with Nevada because he was too young and wild back then. Well she is coming back five years later, Wes said, that's good and I know Nevada will be happy to see her. Shermon said, I hope so Kid.

Then Shermon noticed the two pigs at the far end of the cattle fence. They had already rooted themselves a pig pen. The cowboys had made a pig shelter for the pigs. It was a framed pig house. Shermon said, Kid when you finish with those other 5 cows, it will be supper time, so I will see you at the ranch house.

Reminton met Shermon with the cash box and ledger. KaSandra brought out the large coffee pot and some tin coffee cups. Shermon sat down with his three brothers and they all poured themselves a cup of coffee. Reminton showed Shermon and his other two brother's the ledger. Reminton said, our balance was thirty-six thousand, four hundred, twenty dollars before we spent Two thousand, five hundred dollars for the three thousand, two hundred acres. Now our new balance is Thirty- three thousand, nine hundred, twenty dollars. Shermon said, I would like you three to think about another piece of land for maybe resale at a later time. Lance said, well Sherm you said, resale, so I guess there is money to be made on the land? Shermon said, Lance I can guarantee we will make money on the land. Lance and the other two brothers said, lets go for it.

Shermon said, Like I said before I will be heading out again soon. There are at least 350 to 400 more cows out there for the taking. Plus, there are two young bulls that would be a real prize. Besides the many mustangs. Whatever I don't drive to Eldorado I will bring back here to Autumn's Crossing. Lance asked, how soon are you wanting to leave? Shermon said, as soon as I can put some trail drivers together. Also, we need to have the school house ready for Dawn Marie Adams. I believe I will try to leave right after Dawn Marie arrives and the school house is ready. I will need time to get ready for the drive.

Cap was rigning the dinner bell and yelling come and get it. Shermon said, There is one more thing..... Pass the word that we have a good conestoga covered wagon with a water barrel and two strong oxen for sale. For one price of an even one thousand dollars. Shermon said, after dinner I want to talk to you all about incorporating a canvas over a fold out table at the back of the chuckwagon. Also, some steps into the wagon where we will store food, extra rain gear, blankets and of course ammo and a couple extra guns. I want to make it easy for Cap to go in and out without much trouble with his bad leg.

Cap normally slept under the wagon, but there was plenty of floor space in the wagon for him to sleep if he wanted to. After a good meal Shermon walked over to the bunkhouse where Wes Montana and four other cowboys were sitting on the large front porch. Shermon said, Kid I would like to get the one room school built and then put another trail drive together. I would like to keep the 30 head of branded cattle but take the other 35 head to Eldorado. There is a buyer there that will take all the beef we can get to him and pay good money for them. Then on the way back I would like to bring back those two young bulls that we seen on our last trip, plus some mustangs. I would like to tie up all loose ends here and be ready to leave in about 20 days. Wes Montana said, we will be ready Sherm.

Chapter 18
They Build the School House
And Get Ready for Another Cattle Drive

Shermon asked, Wes Montana, if he could get a couple of the cowboys to break the nine mustang mares and then put the black stallion in the one end of the horse corral with three of the quarter horse mares but leave the other nine quarter horse mares with the nine mustang mares in the larger side of the horse corral. Then for the divided end of the horse corral have all the unsaddle horses. Like the cowboy's horses and Lexi's two horses and any others that are not mustangs or quarter horses. Wes Montana said, they would start on it first thing in the morning after breakfast. Shermon shook Wes Montana's hand and said, Thanks Kid.

The next morning after a good breakfast Shermon seen Harry and Mario and a couple other cowboys quick drawing their guns and Shermon noticed how quick Mario was drawing his gun. Mario reminded him of how fast Wes Montana and Sundance Reid was and he thought he would talk with Mario later. Lance, Wyatt, Jesse, Harry and Mario headed towards town to work on the school house. Wes, Sundance, Blacky and Nevada started breaking horses and moving them to the area that Shermon wanted them to be kept. Logan and Dakota watched the cowboys and knew it wouldn't be long before it would be their turn to break horses and ride the trail.

Shermon then asked Luther Green and Shane Madison to ride with him aways. I would like you two to ride the land. We will build a small but nice shelter for you two to sleep in but if the sun is up you two will be riding the land. One leaves to the east and one leaves to the west then the next day switch the one that rode to the east will ride to the west and the one that rode to the west will ride to the east and you two will switch east and west every day until all our fences are up. Tomorrow morning, I will send two men to the saw mill with you two to mill lumber for the range rovers shack. Those two men will relieve you two every 30 days and then you two will relieve them every 30 days. So, for 30 days you will ride the land and then for 30 days you will work the ranch, okay? Luther and Shane both agreed they would and that they would put their lives on the line if needed. They would ride for the brand. Shermon said, I know you two would, but I hope that it does not come to that.

Shermon then road to where the school house was being built and told Lance and Wyatt of his plans with Luther and Shane and that he was going to talk with Harry and Mario Austin about being the other two range rovers. Lance and Wyatt both thought that it was a good ideal for all four range riders. Shermon talked with Harry and Mario. Both Harry and Mario said that they liked the ideal and that they would ride the range for the McBays now and forever. DRAW MARIO!!! Shermon yelled! Mario drew his gun and it looked like Mario was as fast as Shermon was. But Shermon asked, Mario have you ever shot a man or even drew your gun on a man before. Mario said, I have not, but I will if I have too. Sherm then said, Mario, I believe you would, but I also hope you never have to.

Lance you and Wyatt will have Jesse and Shorty with you starting tomorrow so if you need any more lumber for the school house you might want to get it this afternoon if you can. Tomorrow morning Harry and Mario will be at the sawmill with Luther and Shane they will cut and load the lumber for the range riders shack and then tomorrow morning I will ride out with them and stake a place to build the range riders shack. Harry you and Mario stay with the building of the school house today but tonight you will make plans to be gone a few days building the range riders shack, okay? Harry and Mario both said you got it Sherm. They shook hands and Shermon rode into town.

Earl Scott the marshall walked up to Shermon and asked how everything was going. Shermon said, real good thanks for asking. Marshall Scott then said, I heard Dawn Marie was coming back to town to be the School mom and

I think that is a good thing plus Shermon the things that you and your family have done since you have been here is really a great thing. Marshall I'm glad that you think so, said Shermon.The marshall said, I will see you later Shermon. Then Ringo star the deputy marshall asked Shermon how he was doing as he shook hands with Shermon. Ringo said, I heard about Rick Adams, that's too bad. But I also heard, Dawn Marie was coming back to town to be the school mom? Shermon said, that's right. Ringo asked, did Nevada say anything? Shermon said, I never heard anything, but I believe there's more to it than I know. Ringo said, no problem, Shermon, I will see you later but first, Shermon, you need to see Larry McNally if you want a real large sign. Shermon said thanks Ringo I will go see Larry McNally.

Shermon told Larry McNally that the signs he was looking for was a larger sign saying "Autumn's Crossing" for the ranch then one saying "Waco's School House, dedicated by Caroline Adams" then one for over the door saying "School Teacher, Dawn Marie Adams". Larry McNally said, that he would like to donate the dedicated sign and as far as the door sign it would be $5.00 and then if Shermon would provide and make the lumber the size of the sign he wanted for Autumn's Crossing, Larry said he would letter it for $30.00. Shermon agreed to it and asked Larry McNally to start on the signs as soon as he could. Larry said they won't take to long to make. Shermon then headed for Autumn's Crossing.

Everyone was busy. The smoker was smoking with good smelling beef jerky. Wes Montana and his cowboys were breaking wild mustang mares and they had all the horses separated like Shermon had asked. As Shermon pulled up Wes said, that black stallion has already mounted two of those quarter horses and is about to mount the third. That's good Shermon said, lets leave them 3 quarter horses in there with him for a couple days to make sure it takes. Where is Cap, Shermon asked? Wes Montana said, he is doing something to the chuck wagon.

Shermon started towards the chuck wagon when Cheyenne stepped out onto the covered porch. So as Shermon rode by he put out his hand and Cheyenne took it and then the next thing she was on Shermon's lap and neither buck nor Shermon complained about it. Cheyenne kissed Shermon and asked, how are you doing big man? I'm doing a lot better now that you are here with me but…. Cheyenne said, that's good to hear, but what is the but?? Well me and some cowboys are taking some lumber about 15 miles from here tomorrow morning to start a range rovers shack. Cheyenne asked how long will you be gone? Well only a couple days on this trip, but then after that I am going to trail some beef to Eldorado and bring back some mustangs and maybe a couple bulls. Cheyenne looked a little sad. Shermon said, I'm sorry to be leaving but I am doing this for all of us and soon I won't have to be gone as much. Cheyenne said, well I signed on for it. So, I will be here when you return. And they kissed long and hard. Cheyenne slipped down off Shermon's lap and said, I'm here when you are ready Sherm. Shermon said, thanks for understanding.

Cap crawled out of the chuck wagon and asked when are we leaving boss? Well it will be a week to 10 days when we hit the trail to Eldorado again, but I am going to ride out in the morning for two days with four cowboys. What will you need Cap asked? We will be taking lumber to build a range rovers base camp about 15 miles from here. Harry, Mario, Luther, Shane and I, will leave in two days. Harry and Mario will stay while the shack is being built then come back. The four of them will be switching off every 30 days for a couple months or more. I am riding with the four to pick out a spot for the range rovers shack and then I will head back the next morning. Cap said, I will have a coffee pot and skillet plus another pot ready for the trip. I will send plenty of beans smoked bacon and beef jerky plus of course coffee. That will be good Shermon said. There is plenty of small game plus a good stream where they can get good cold water. Shermon said, Cap, if you will get that ready so we can take it with us that would be great. Cap asked, anything else boss? Shermon said, as soon as we can we will trail to Eldorado again. The trip will take 4 to 5 weeks and I hope no more. So then you can have the chuck wagon loaded for a six week trail drive if you will Cap? Cap said, you got it boss.

Shermon sat down and was drinking a cup of coffee. Reminton came up and Shermon poured Reminton a cup of coffee and asked Reminton, what was on his mind? Reminton said, Shermon I think we are really moving fast and maybe a lot faster than we thought. I am not complaining I was just wondering, how big are we going to be? Shermon said, Reminton we have our original, six thousand, four hundred acres plus the three thousand, two hundred acres and if we buy the other three thousand, two hundred acres we will have a total of twelve thousand, eight hundred acres. That would support all our horses, and whatever cows we have without need of buying other food for our stock. Shermon said, Reminton if everyone is in favor of buying the three thousand, two hundred acres then after the trail drive we will look in to it.

The next morning Shermon asked, Harry, Mario, Shane and Luther if they were ready to build a rover's shack. Shermon said we will pick out a good spot and then I will head back to Autumn's Crossing. Late that day they found a great spot for the Rover's shack. Shermon said, lets have some coffee and a biscuit we will stake the corners for the shack in the morning. The next morning while drinking coffee Shermon said, that water in the stream is good and cold Luther said, I know it's cold, I threw some on my face this morning. Harry said, I notice a lot of fox squirrels in those trees. Shermon said, there sure is plus rabbits and I even seen some pheasants in that tall grass. Luther said, theres duck eggs and ducks at the water's edge plus dear scrapings Harry said, we will eat good when not riding the line. Shermon said, if you don't it will be your own fault. We always need to live off the land when we can. Then Shermon headed back to Autumn's crossing.

Shermon rode up to the smoker and hung the buck on the side of the smoker and asked Wes Montana, to have a couple of the cowboys build a fire and smoke the large buck that he shot on the way back. Cut the back strap out and then the shoulders and then if you will smoke the rest of the deer Shermon said, to Kid. After checking inside, I am going to ride over to see how the school house is coming along. Shermon walked in the ranch house and Cheyenne handed him a tin cup full of hot black coffee. Now that's worth the trip he said, and Cheyenne asked, Me or the coffee big man? Well of course you Cheyenne, but the coffee is pretty good also and laughed. Cheyenne and Shermon hugged and Shermon asked Cheyenne if she wanted to ride with him to see the school house. Cheyenne said, give me 5 minutes big man. Shermon asked, Wes Montana to have one of the cowboys to saddle Button's, Cheyenne's horse. Cheyenne had named her horse Buttons because it was a chestnut horse with what looked like a row of buttons from front to back.

Shermon was talking with Wes Montana, Blacky Moore and Nevada Smith when Cheyenne walked out on the porch. All three men quit talking. Cheyenne asked, hey big man did I do something wrong? Cheyenee's red auburn hair was blowing in the breeze and she looked so pretty wih her long legs in her tight fitting jeans and all the right curves and her small waist which gave her the hour glass figure and of course the white shirt with the two top buttons unbuttoned did not hurt because it revealed the top of some real nice looking breasts. After a moment Shermon said, No Cheyenne you did everything just right. Are you redy to head out Shermon asked? Yes, I am Cheyenne said. Shermon said, we will be back by supper time, Kid, and we will bring some hungry men with us.

Shermon and Cheyenne rode through town and to the site where the one room school house was being built. Lance, Wyatt, Jesse and Shorty were on the roof and Harry and Mario was handing up boards for them to nail in place. Shermon said, you men are doing good and it looks like you are ahead of where we had hoped to be at this time. Lance climbed down off the roof and said, well everything is going real good and I have some real good carpenters here. Shermon said it shows for sure and it looks like maybe 3 or 4 more days, Jesse said, Sherm, I think 3 days the most.

While they were talking, Larry McNally, pulled up in a small wagon. Larry said Shermon, I have the two signs for the school house. But the large one you might want to pick up with this larger wagon on your way back to your ranch. That's fine Larry lets see the two you have for the school house. Larry pulled out the larger Waco's School house sign dedicated by Caroline Adams and Shermon said, Larry dedicated the cost of this sign and the school was dedicated by Caroline Adams, husband, Rick Adams. Then Larry showed them the door sign which said School Mom, Dawn Marie Adams. Wyatt said, these are two nice signs but what is the third sign Sherm? Shermon said, it is kind of a surprise, but I will tell you it is a sign for the ranch. I can hardly wait to see it Wyatt said. Shermon said me and Cheyenne will see you all back at Autumn's Crossing. We need to go next door to the general store first.

Shermon and Cheyenne went into the general store. Shermon asked Micka and Daniel Grant what the tally looked like for this month. I want to make sure the bill is paid every month and we can pay it weekly if need be Shermon said. Daniel said looks like cut nails, rope and a few other dry goods. The total is not much currently. Micka said, we aren't worried about you all paying. Shermon said, we don't want to tie up to much of your money just let me know if you want us to pay more often than monthly.

While Shermon was talking with the Grants, Cheyenne walked out on the boardwalk out front of the general store and sat down on the bench. There was a very large man sitting on a mule and Cheyenne looked away but thought he was still staring at her. Cheyenne tried not to look his way she knew he was trouble as soon as she seen him. Cheyenne had wished she had stayed inside but the cigar smoke was more than she could handle by the two men inside. But then as Shermon stepped out of the general store onto the boardwalk. The large mountain man, said, nice looking legs red, What time do they open? That's all it took. Shermon took two steps and he was standing on the top of the hitching rail then Shermon flew off the hitching rail into the mountain man, driving the big man to the ground real hard. But surprisingly the mountain man was right back on his feed and circling Shermon. The way the mountain man moved you could tell he was an Indian fighter. He was very cocky and sure of himself.

The mountain man's legs were like tree trunks Shermon knew that he was going to be in for a fight and also knew that there was no way that he would be able to keep the mountain man on his back without knocking him out some-how. But the big guy was rude and Shermon would not tolerate it. Cheyenne noticed a crowd growing then she seen Lance, Wyatt, Jesse and Ringo stand-ing in the crowd. Cheyenee seen the scalp's hanging on the mountain mans saddle. Shermon did not see anyone but the large mountain man in front of him. All Shermon could think of was Cheyenne's honor was at stake and he was not going to cotton to it. The mountain man came at Shermon and as they went down Shermon was on top, but the large man threw Shermon off and laughed out loud. They both were on their feet and circling each other.

The big man came at Shermon fast. Shermon hit him with a right cross and then a left hook. Shermon came around with a round house that hardly moved the large mountain man. Shermon thought to himself, this man is no quitter. The mountain man reached out and drew Shermon to him. But as he did Shermon hit him twice. The big man still got Shermon in a front bear hug. Shermon's feet were off the ground. Shermon brought both fists down hard to his forehead. Then Shermon hit the big man with an uppercut and then another one. Shermon broke loose for only a couple of seconds as the big man tried to take Shermon to the ground. Shermon head butted the mountain man and as they were still going down Shermon brought up his knee and drove it to the big man's crotch. The mountain man grabbed his crotch with both hands. Shermon hit the big man in his throat with a very hard open palm. Then Sher-mon came around with an elbow to the big mans nose they both had blood on them and you could not tell whose blood it was. But the big man was on his back with his knees bent and was groaning plus he was spitting blood and holding his testicles. Shermon was barely standing but said, I won't tolerate rude people.

Lance and Wyatt went to help Shermon on his horse buck. Shermon waved them back and said, if I can't get on my horse then I deserve to walk. Shermon made it to bucks saddle and headed buck towards Autumn's Crossing. The street was still full of people they all were clapping and yelling way to go Shermon. Cheyenne and the others rode on both sides of Shermon even though they knew he would not accept any help. Marshall Scott and Ringo helped Jack Turner the mountain man to his feet and asked him if he was okay. Jack turner said, who in the hell was that guy. Ringo said, that was Shermon McBay and he will not tolerate rude people. Turner said, that is the first time I ever got whipped in a fight. Ringo said, well you were whipped, weren't you? Jack Turner the big mountain man said, Shermon McBay you say, well I like that Shermon McBay. He's got a mean streak and as soon as I can I am going to tell him so. Ringo said, I think I would give Shermon a couple days to cool down. Jack turner said, Deputy you are probably right. Would you tell Shermon that he is okay with me. Tell him I live in the hills and when I get the chance I will try and make it up to him for being rude. Turner said, see you and rode off wiping blood from his nose.

Chapter 19
Shermon and his cowboys
get ready to hit the trail

When Shermon and the rest rode into Autumn's Crossing, Reminton and Wes Montana was the first to notice Shermon. As Shermon dismounted Buck he slipped and almost went to his knees. Reminton and Wes both grabbed for Shermon. Shermon waved them back as he said, I'm okay. Cheyenne said, you were in a hell of a fight, let them help you, big man. Shermon said, I'll be okay, let me sit here on this chunk of wood a minute, as he sat down on a tree stump.

Cheyenne went in the ranch house and came out with Cap and KaSandra, who had some towels and warm water. KaSandra started wiping Shermons face and said, I think Sherm needs a few stitches. Cap said, let me look at him. Then Cap said, Let's get Shermon in the shade. Cap then said, boss you need a few stitches over your right eye and a couple on your left cheek under your left eye. He said, Sherm the way you look, I would hate to see the other guy. Cheyenne said, it was some fight, but Shermon Won!! Shermon said, I will be okay. Cap said, you will boss, but I need to put a few stitches on two of those cuts, if you will let me. Cheyenne said, you will let him wont you, Shermon? Shermon said, well let's get on with it I got a lot of work to do.

So, under the shade of the porch Cap put five stitches above Shermons right eye and two stitches under his left eye. Cap then asked, anything else hurting boss? Cheyenne handed Shermon a tin cup of black coffee. Shermon said, I'm sure everything hurts but now with these stitches and black coffee I will be fine. Shermon said, thanks to Cap and to Cheyenne, then KaSandra asked, when did this fight happened. Who was there and what caused the fight? Reminton said, I hate to say this big brother, but it looks like you might have fell off buck and then buck walked on you a couple of times.

Lance said, Reminton you mentioned Buck, well that montain man Shermon whipped was the biggest man I've ever seen. Lance said, the mountain man Sherm whipped was as big as buck and maybe as heavy as buck also. Then Wes Asked was he riding a mule? Wyatt said, he sure was. Then Wes and Sundance Reid, both said, at the same time, that was Jack Turner. Sundance said, I sure would have liked to have seen Shermon whip Jack Turner. That big mountain man is or can be a real nice guy if he wants to be but you get him mad and look out. It normally takes 4 or 5 men to slow Jack Turner down and tie him up. Then Wes asked, why did you have to whip him Sherm? Shermon said, Kid he was rude to Cheyenne. Then Shermon said, you know Kid, I can't tolerate rude people. They all said, we know that Sherm. Dakota said, Uncle Sherm I don't blame you I won't tolerate it either. Then Ringo rode up to where Shermon was sitting on the porch. Ringo said, Shermon how are you? That sure was a hell of a fight. Then Ringo said, Jack Turner asked me to tell you he was sorry that he was rude to your woman.

After a good supper and an early night Shermon felt a little better and he told Wes Montana so. Shermon was sitting on his heels and pouring himself a cup of coffee and Wes said, Sherm you still look like a herd of cattle run over you. Shermon said, Kid I guess I look like I feel. Wes poured himself a cup of coffee and poured Shermon another cup. Wes said, Shermon you could have not picked a meaner person than mountain man Jack Turner. Shermon said, Kid I did not pick him. He picked me when he was rude to Cheyenne. Then shermon said, the talking was done. Shermon said, but I will say I would like to have him on our side if we meet him again. But it will be up to him.

Shermon said, well Kid, we have some ends to tie up before we can leave. Then Harry and Mario rode into Autumn's Crossing. Harry looked at Shermon and asked, Sherm, did you tangle with a bear? Wes said, it might as well have been a bear, it was mountain man, Jack turner.Mario said, I sure wish I was there to see Shermon whip Jack Turner, Harry said, so do I. Jack Turner, WOW! Reminton said, Shermon why don't you take the day off. Shermon said, the fight is over and now I have work that needs to be done. Shermon asked, how does the line shack look? Mario said, it looks good. It does not look like a shack. Mario poured himself a cup of coffee plus he poured a cup for Harry also.

Shermon asked Wes Montana to get the rest of the cowboys. Shermon said, we need to make a list of trail drivers and a list of cowboys staying here. Harry I would like you and Mario to relieve Luther and Shane in 30 days as planned. Then they can check in with Reminton when they return to Autumns Crossing. Okay cowboys going on the trail. Cap with the chuck wagon, Kid, Blacky, Sundance, What about you Nevada? Do you want to go or stay? Nevada Smith said, of course, I'll go, Shermon, me and Dawn Marie is over, it's the past, plus Dawn Marie likes Ringo Starr and I think he would be good for her. Shermon said, Nevada you are on the trail drive now I need a couple more and how about Logon and Dakota? Dakota and Logon both jumped up and asked, do you mean it Uncle Sherm? Well I talked with your mom and dad and they all thought it would be a good ideal. So, Dakota and Logon you both will be on the payroll and I expect you both to earn it. Logon and Dakota, both said you can count on me Uncle Sherm. Okay, then there is eight of us going on the trail and at leaset five men at the ranch and two range riding. Does anyone have anything to add? Dakota said, do I get to wear my .44 colt and my bowie knife? Shermon said, you sure do Dakota. Logon asked, when do we leave Uncle Sherm? Well how about in two days, we will pull out Monday at high noon then we can stay at the line shack Monday night and then head out Tuesday at sun up. Wes, if you will go with Dakota and Logon and help them pick out two horses. Shermon said Dakota and Logon I want you two to always remember your horse will be as good to you as you are to your horse. Dakota and Logon both said, we will be real good to our horse. Okay both of you cowboys make sure you have your extra gear at the back of the chuck wagon by the end of the day. If you are not sure of what to take, see Kid or Cap and they will help this first trip.

Then Shermon said, we will be leaving in two days so do what you need to do today. If anyone needs a cash allowance, see Reminton today. The rest of your pay will be paid when we return after the trail drive. So, enjoy your day but we are leaving at noon Monday. Shermon then asked, Reminton are you

planning on building a black smith shop with indoor horse stalls and a large
tack room and loft while we are gone? Reminton said, we should either be
done with it or close to being done when you return. Then Lance walked up
and poured a cup of coffee. So, if you lay out the black smith shop with horse
stalls on both sides and large doors on both ends make sure you leave room for
a good size tack room and maybe a loft on both sides above the horse stalls for
hay storage. Later we will build a shelter for only hay storage. Lance this will
be your operation. Have Jesse help you with the help of others and try to stay
close to the drawings that we went over.

Reminton if you will keep shorty at the sawmill with Wyatt cutting lumber
I think Shorty is better at the sawmill but Wyatt the saw mill is your operation. So just keep cutting lumber if you will unless Reminton needs you at the
ranch for a couple days. Shermon said, that he was going to town and asked
Cheyenne if she would want to go. Cheyeynne asked, are you planning on
whipping anyone today big man? Shermon said, I would like to heal a couple
days before I run into another rude person but if someone needs whipped I will
whip him. Cheyenne said, let me get buttons. Wes Montana said, I will saddle
buttons Cheyenne. Cheyenne said, thanks Kid.

Then KaSandra was on the porch and said hey if you two don't mind me
and Reminton will to go town with you. Shermon said, if you two would like
to go with us you sure can. You are always welcome to go plus anyone else
that needs to go to town. Reminton saddled him and KaSandras a horse while
KaSandra went in to change.

When KaSandra and Cheyenne stepped back out onto the porch they almost looked like twins. They both had tight fitting jeans on and you know they
fit them like socks on a turkey. They both had white shirts on that had the top
two buttons unbuttoned that looked just right. They had their colt .44's belted
on their hips plus a small bowie knife. Reminton said, well I'll be, will you
look at those two. Shermon said, I am looking Rem. Cheyenne and KaSandra
asked, do we look okay or do you want us to change? Shermon and Reminton
both said, don't change a thing. We like you two just as you are. Cheyenne
said, thanks Big man.

As the four rode into town, Ringo called to Shermon. Ringo said, Dawn
Marie is over at the general store. She would like to meet you Shermon plus
the rest of your family. We want to meet her also, Shermon said. They tied
their horses to the hitching rail anyway, Shermon just let buck's lay over the

hitching rail but the other three tied theirs to the hitching rail. Shermon said, buck will stay here unless I call or whistle for him. When they walked into the general store Dawn Marie said Ringo you don't have to introduce me to Shermon because I would know him anywhere. Dawn Marie shook hands with all four and mentioned how nice Cheyenne and KaSandra looked. Dawn Marie thanked Shermon for his help with her brother and the one room school house, she said how she was looking forward to being the teacher. Then she said how much she liked the one room school house, plus her name sign over the door.

Cheyenne and KaSandra noticed how young and thin and also how pretty Dawn Marie was. Shermon asked, Dawn Marie, is there anything else that you might need? Dawn Marie said, I don't think so or how about maybe a school bell? Then Micka and Daniel Grant held up the bell that Shermon had ordered. Shermon said, lets go put it on the school house. Shermon asked, Dawn Marie, where he should mount the bell then Shermon said, Try the bell out. Dawn Marie pulled the rawhide. The bell was loud but had a very nice sound. Dawn Marie hugged all four of them Dawn Marie had tears in her eyes and told them they were happy tears. Ringo said, I will see all of you later and shook Shermon and Reminton's hands.

Shermon said, lets go back to the general store and drop off this list. Let's take just what we need for now and ask Micka if he could have the rest to Autumn's Crossing in the morning. Micka said it will be there by sunup if you want it so. Shermon said, it doesn't have to be by sunup, but we will need some of the items before noon. Micka said it will be there in the morning.

As they were leaving town KaSandra said those chicken eggs were twenty cents a dozen. Daniel said, they could sell a lot more if they had them. Reminton asked, what are you getting at? KaSandra said, we buy a lot of eggs and Lisa Potter buys a lot for her café but Daniel said, they don't have eggs to sell most of the time. Shermon then asked KaSandra are you saying that we should have chickens? KaSandra said not only could we eat a few of the chickens but the eggs we don't eat we could surely sell. Shermon said, okay if you women want to sell eggs and a few chickens then I guess we should order some baby chicks but no more pigs. But remember me and my cowbys won't have time to gather any eggs. Also, Rem I guess you need to put a chicken coop on your list. What do you think about that rocky area that probably would make a great place for a chicken coop and pen.

Shermon asked Cheyenne and KaSandra if they knew what they needed. KaSandra asked could you give us some pointers? Shermon said, well if you want to sell chickens you will need a rooster, so the eggs will become chicks. Or you could sell your chickens every couple years, and then buy more. Without a rooster your eggs wont, be fertile. The women agreed that they wanted a rooster. Because they wanted to sell eggs plus a few chickens. Shermon said, Reminton you have your work cut out for you. Cheyenne said, we can help build the chicken coop. KaSandra said, you know we can. Shermon said, Well Reminton it looks like you will have another project. Can you work it in with the blacksmith shop and the barb wire fence? Reminton said, we should be okay with all the good help we have to get the work done. KaSandra and Cheyenne could hardly wait to tell Abigail, Brandy and the three girls about the chickens.

When they pulled up to Autumn's Crossing Cap and Kid Montana was waiting to talk with Shermon and Lance told Shermon that he had some questions also. Shermon said, what's your question Cap? Cap said, I just need to know how many days of supplies should I figure on? Shermon said, lets take enough for 8 weeks. Then whatever we are short on for the trip back we will get at Eldorado. Cap then asked what about floor space? Shermon said, I don't think we will need very much floor space, let's just take and extra tarp. Also, Cap, lets take plenty of ammo and that buffalo gun with some shells.

Then Shermon asked Lance, what was on his mind? Lance said, Sherm, we talked about access to the roof from the tack room to the loft. But I was wondering if you thought the area that we use should all be concealed? Shermon said, that's a good question Lance. I think it should be concealed from the tack room to the roof. We can use a pull down ladder and a trap door. I hope we don't ever have to use it. But it will be handy to have if we ever do need it. Also, Sherm we never mentioned how many stalls we wanted to have in the black smith shop? Shermon said, with all the room that we will have let's start out with 18 and make 4 of those that could be used as doubles.

Shermon turned towards Wes Montana. Okay, Kid, thanks for waiting. What's on your mind? Wes Montana said, Sherm, I laid out the 3 strain fence for the cattle and it's twice as long as it is wide. But I need to know about gates. Where and how big do you want the gates? Shermon said, even though it will be just a holding pen. I think we should have a double gate on the far end and also a good size gate on the outside of the fenced in area towards the lake, down where the water leaves the lake, but where the cattle won't have access to the lake. Wes Montana said, that sounds real good. Shermon said, Kid just pass that onto Jesse, let him know and he will take care of the gates. Kid I would like for you to come back and see me as soon as you can. I would like to talk to you about Dakota and Logon. Wes said, I will be right back Sherm.

When Wes got back, he poured himself a cup of coffee. Wes then asked, Whats up Sherm? Shermon started out, well Kid I want you to help me watch Dakota and Logon. I don't want to treat them like boys, but there is a lot that can go wrong on a trail drive. I know it and so do you. I don't ever want to sound negative, but I do want to keep them as safe as we can while they pull their own weight. Wes said, Sherm, Mario has worked with them on throwing a rope. They have really picked it up and are pretty good, plus me and Mario both have worked with them with their colts. You could tell that Reminton had worked with them before because they are pretty good, Sherm. Sherm said, Kid did you tell them that being fast with a draw was good but hitting what you shoot at could make the difference? Wes said, Shermon I told them that it did not matter how fast you where. If you did not hit where you were aiming. Sherm said, thanks Kid. I know you will help me get them back home safe. Wes Montana said, I also went over their gear with Cap and them. I told them, bed rolls, raingear, extra canteen and beef jerky needed to be as important as their horse and their Colt .44.

Chapter 20
Shermon and his 7 Cowboys hit the trail

The next morning, they all had a good breakfast. Shermon went down a checklist, he did it mainly for Dakota and Logon but every one of the cowboys followed Shermon's lead. They all checked their gear. Bedrolls, raingear, extra canteen, they checked their Colt .44, their repeating rifle and their ammo. Shermon, Dakota and Logon hugged all the women and shook hands with all the men. Everyone was proud, but mostly Dakota and Logon had the proudest look on their faces you would ever see. Shermon winked at his family standing in front of them. There were eight cowboys sitting tall, 7 cowboys sitting on saddles and one cowboy sitting on the seat of the chuckwagon. Shermon said, Let's roll out. Shermon said to Kid, Dakota and Logon, might be a little nervous but they will do whatever they have to no matter what it might be. Every cowboy was saying a little prayer to themselves and the family watching the cowbys was holding hands and also praying as the cowboys moved out of sight.

As they pulled up to the line shack Shermon said to Dakota and Logon, do you two think that you could maybe shoot 5 or 6 squirrels? Dakota said, me and Logon seen quite a few squirrels in those nut trees, so I don't see why we couldn't shoot 5 or 6. Shermon said, good 5 or 6 will be plenty. I will ask Cap to cut up some potatoes and make a squirrel stew. As Dakota and Logon were heading back with the squirrels they seen Luther and Shane. Luther said, we heard the shooting and we new it was someone shooting squirrels. Dakota said, they are for a squirrel stew. Shane said, that sounds good.

Then Luther asked Shermon, I thought you were going to take half of the cows to Eldorado? Shermon said, there was a change of plans. Looks like we will have a horse ranch and a cattle ranch. Dakota said, Uncle Sherm, don't forget, also a chicken Ranch and Logon said and a pig ranch too. Shermon laughed and said just the 2 pigs for now. Yea Dakota, I guess the women will have some chickens and some eggs but us men will have horses and cows.

Luther said, I will help you skin them squirrels and cut them up. Shane said, I will get a fire going. Shermon said, I hope you two have some coffee cooking. Luther said, Sorry, Sherm but we drank what we had made. Cap said, lets get this fire going and we will have plenty of coffee in no time. By the time the squirrels were ready, and the potatoes cut for the stew the coffee was hot and ready. Cap put the squirrel pieces and the cut potatoes in a large pot with other secret items over the fire to cook. Cap made biscuits in a dutch oven. Then a little later Shermon said, that sure was a good meal Cap. Luther and Shane plus Blacky was still dipping their biscuits in the stew and shaking their heads, yes, it was really good.

Shermon was looking at the post that Luther and Shane had in the ground for the Corral. Shermon asked his cowboys if anyone wanted to help him put up the rails and in no time the horse corral was finished. Shermon said, Luther you and Shane can build the gate when you get a chance. Shermon said, you cowboys can stay up as long as you want, but I am going to get some shuteye. We will be leaving right after breakfast.

The next morning Shermon rolled out of his bedroll. Cap was already cooking breakfast, the coffee is ready Sherm, do you want to eat now or wait boss? Shermon said, I'm ready. Then Wes walked up and said I'm ready also. Then one by one the cowboys showed up and grabbed a plate. Cap said, there is biscuits, smoked bacon, cut potatoes and 4 eggs a piece. Cap said, there is a box of tin cups for the coffee. After breakfast, Cap said, throw your tin plates and cups in that box. Then Cap went over and washed them in the stream and then put them back in the wagon for the next meal. Dakota handed Cap the large pot and the dutch oven and Cap said, thanks as he put them up. Shermon was looking the line shack over and said, Mario said, this wasn't a shack and he was right, it really looks good.

Shermon told everyone that he had a couple things to say about the trail, before heading out. Kid Montana and the other cowboys knew what Shermon was about to say was for Dakota and Logon more than them. But Wes Montana and the other older cowboys either sat or stood around while Shermon was talking. Shermon said, first I have always felt that where ever I took my boots off, I belonged there. But always turn your boots upside down and hit them together before putting them back on your feet. Where we are going there will be scorpions and at night they will crawl into your boots so make sure you turn your boots upside down and hit them together before pulling your boots back on. Also, at night, keep your bedrools back from the light of the fire. Lay your bedrools in the shadows, also walk in the shadows. Don't be a target for an Indian or a badman laying in the trees. Don't ever ride into camp without first sayhing hello in the camp real loud. This trail should not be to bad, but every day may not be as good as we would like it to be. I hope we can find something good in everyday. There will be times that you will have to follow your heart but take your brain with you. Never ride out alone in a low area or into the trees by yourself. Always flank the cattle or horses by being on the outside, you won't get trapped on the inside. Your horse could go down or you could get thrown off your horse. The cattle could start running. We all need to watch out for the other cowboy and to remind them to stay alert and never chase a cow or horse without being able to see for aways. We don't want to be a target for Indians or bad men. So, I hope we can count our rainbows and not count our thunder storms. We all want to get back home safe. So, keep reminding yourself and the other cowboys. So, lets pray to God to keep us safe and lets roll out.

Shermon told Dakota and Logon to ride on the right side of the chuckwagon with him and Kid Montana. Shermon told Sundance, Nevada and Blacky to ride the left side of the chuck wagon. Kid, Shermon said, we should start seeing some beef and we will pick them up as we go. I hope those two young bulls are still up ahead where we seen them last time. Wes Montana said, lets hope they are and that they did not get shot by an Indian or someone else. If we see them Kid, I would like to leave them now and pick them up on the way back to Autumn's Crossing. Wes asked, Sherm, how many head do you hope to pick up? Kid, I'm thinking maybe 300 but maybe a little more or a little less. But what we don't take to Eldorado, we might pick up on the way back to Autumn's Crossing. I'm really hoping to take them two young angus bulls and a few beefs and some horses back to the ranch on our way back.

Then Dakota said, Look, Uncle Sherm, at that white stallion running with all those Mustang Mares. That's the horse that I hope to have someday. Sherm said, we will see what we can do on the way back Dakota. Then off to their left there was maybe 18 or 20 head of cattle. Let's bring these cows up to our trail and then watch for more Shermon said. The cowboys pulled a small circle from the chuck wagon then came back to the wagon with 20 head of cattle. Dakota said, that was easy!! Wes Montana said, Yea, Dakota that was easy, but I am afraid that they all won't be that easy. Then Nevada Smith said, and the horses will run hard when we try to pick them off the trail but that is in a cowboy's day and if they did not run we would not want them. It is just like a woman who can not cook. No body wants her and Nevada Laughed and then they picked up about 30 more cows before they seen the two young bulls. They were really starting to grow.

Shermon said, maybe we had better take these two bulls with us. They probably will follow these cows and we won't have to worry about them getting shot or not being here when we return. So, with very little coaching the two bulls fell in with the small group of cows. That's good Shermon said, because it won't be long before these two young bulls will be thinking of nothing but breeding and I hope we will have them back to Autumn's Crossing when that time comes. Dakota asked, Uncle Sherm, I know that those bulls are bulls, but why do they look so much different from them longhorns? Well Dakota, Shermon said, those two are angus bulls and William Handcock had the same ideal as us to make a bigger and stronger beef by breeding the young angus bulls to the long horns. Mr. Handcock told me before he died what he had in mind before he got hurt and then he just did not care to go on. He told me that he was done and good luck to me then he drank himself to death.

Wes Said, Sherm there's those two stallions and that larger group of mares and the white Stalion is over there also. Lets just leave them alone for now. We will concentrate on the cattle and then on the way back the horses. Shermon said, Kid that's is a real good looking spot over there for Camp. Wes Said, yea looks like we can bed down on that knoll under those couple of oak trees and maybe keep the cattle in that shallow base below us. Plus look at all that deadwood. Shermon said yea, and if we do it just right the smoke will drift up into those trees without causing too much of a smoke trail. Wes said, are you thinking about Indians Sherm? Ive seen a couple of signs of Indians haven't you? Sherm, asked Kid Montana? Kid said, I've seen some but I thought they were crossing in front of us. But, if it's one thing I know about Indians it is that you can't count on them to do what you expect them to do.

They pulled in on the knoll and bedded the cattle in the base below the knoll. Sundance started gathering some deadwood with Nevada. Wes Montana showed Dakota and Logon how to water the horses from a very small trickle of water at the base of the knoll. Wes said, we have plenty of water but always use any other water when possible. After all, 8 horses drank, Wes took a shovel from the chuckwagon and in no time there was a pretty good size watering hole. They picketed the horses and let the two oxen get a good drink and then all the cattle were drinking and after a short time the cattle were all laying down. The fire was going, and the coffee pot was full of hot black coffee. Cap handed Dakota and Logon 8 tin cups and asked them to hand them out. Cap had a real good super ready in no time. Beans, smoked bacon, biscuits and black coffee. They all ate their fill.

Shermon said, I believe we have Indians out there and they know we are here, so I want everyone here to know that they are out there. We need to keep our guard up starting tonight we will start night guard and I will tell you all that there has been more cowboys killed by Indians while they had their pants down doing there morning dump than there has been shot off their horses. So be alert and ready at all times. Wes Montana said, Sherm, Logon here said, he was ready to stay up all night on guard duty. So, if you want me and Logon to, we will take first watch. Shermon said, sure and how about you, Cap and Blacky relieving them in a couple hours and then, Sundance you and Nevada take the last night guard here at camp? Dakota and I, will bed down over there at the willow tree and I will take buck and he will let us know if anything comes our way. They grabbed their bedrolls and Shermon and Dakota headed to the other side of the cattle to bed down under the willow.

You know why I picked this spot Dakota, Shermon asked? Well I think because we can see the cattle and camp real good from here Uncle Sherm. You are right about being able to see the cattle an the camp, but we are also in the shadows under this tree and if those 182 beef decided to run and they came our way we have this large tree to protect us from getting run over, by the cattle, plus the large limbs with all the small limbs give us some shelter but mostly the shadow will help us from being seen so easy, and buck will warn us if anyone or anything trys to sneak up on us. So before you fall a sleep what are you going to listen to Shermon asked Dakota? Dakota said, I am going to listen to all the night sounds like you told me about on our trail from Kansas to Waco, Texas. Then I will know if I hear other noises in the night that they are noises that I did not hear earlier and that they are noises that I should not be hearing now, Right Uncle Sherm? That's right Dakota, I am glad that you remember because it could keep you alive some night. Always be alert and having a horse like buck does not hurt either, because he will always let me know even before something or someone gets close to me. Yea Uncle Sherm, some day my White Horse might do the same for me. Well after we breed it to three or four of those quarter horse mares and then we casterate the Stallion then you can work with the horse without him trying to kill you. But before that every-one will have to stay clear of him but after he's caterated then you will have to earn his trust and I know you will put in the time to make him your horse while you both are still young. Now lets try to get a little shut eye.

Thanks Uncle Sherm! For what Dakota, Shermon asked? For being my uncle and the white stallion. Dakota you will earn that horse I guarantee it. Then Shermon heard Dakota praying: Now I lay me down to sleep, I pray the Lord my soul to keep. If I die before I wake, I pray the lord my soul to take. P.S. Lord please take care of Uncle Sherm and all his cowboys including me, and Logon also please watch over everyone back home oh yea if you will help me with the white stallion. In Jesus name, Amen! Shermon said, Amen and smiled and closed his eyes.

Shermon talked to buck a couple times in the night. Buck would snort threw his nostrils and make a little noise. But his head never came up and he never stamped his feet so Shermon knew if bucks ears never came up to sound an alarm nothing ever got close enough for Shermon to worry about. The next morning Wes told Shermon that he had heard something big moving in the trees and Shermon told Wes that he had also heard it and after some coffee and a biscuit he was going to scout over that way. Kid you can ride over there with me if you want. Wes said, I think we should while these beefs are eating on that buffalo grass. Shermon told Cap and the rest of the cowboys to get ready to pull out.

So, while camp was being cleared and the cowboys were watering the horses and hooking the 2 oxen to the wagon, Wes Montana and Shermon rode over to the tree line. Buck plus Kids horse (Black Jack) both were a little skittish as they got closer to the tree line. Then Shermon and Kid both heard the breaking of the small trees and seen the tall grass laying down as the largest bear they ever seen came crashing towards them. The bear was showing his teeth and was growling so loud that the cowboys hardly heard the gun's being fired. But luckily Shermon had his rifle ready and told Wes to be ready. Then the large bear stood up and Shermon and Wes both fired at the same time.

Then Wes told Shermon here's why that bear was so angry with us. That bear had a freshly killed buck he was trying to defend from us. Wes said, I am going to cut the back strap and some shoulder meat off. Shermon said, lets do it quick. So as Wes climbed down from black jack Shermon stood guard. Shermon then said, Kid, we need to move out as soon as possible. I don't believe this was the only bear out here look at all these bear tracks. Wes said, let me put this meat in this sack cloth and then we will ride out. As Shermon and Wes Montana rode back into their camp and Shermon said, Hello in the camp, All the cowboys asked what was over there? Shermon said, it was a large bear. Wes Montana handed the sack cloth to Cap and said, here is some very fresh deer meat. Cap said, good and rinsed it off and put some salt on the meat and hung it up in the wagon.

Then Cap said, this will be supper tomorrow and tomorrow is Sunday. As they were pulling away, Shermon looked back over towards the tree line and seen two more large bears. Shermon said, we will have to remember this bear country on the way back. Wes said, there's one less bear to worry about now and I hope we don't run into anymore. We will stay clear of that tree line on the way back I believe that them bears just wait for their meals to come to them. So, they can have that tree line.

Then they spotted about 20 head of cattle off to the left as they moved away from the trees. Dakota said, well these cows stayed clear of them bears didn't' they? Logon said, yea, so I guess that cows aren't to stupid after all. No one else said anything but all the cowboys where hoping not to see any more bears. The cowboys picked up the 20 head of beefs then within no time they had about 20 more then they got another 15 before they stopped for the night a long way from the bear area.

They pulled up to a knoll with a couple good size trees and there was good water and good grass. They watered the horses and the cows drank water and ate grass but stayed close together. The two young bulls were content with things, so they just laid down where they were. While Cap was getting supper together Sundance and Nevada were restacking the stones that had been used before by other cowboys and started a fire with deadwood and even some buffalo chips. The smoke was drifting upwards into the trees but the view was real good from all four sides and you could not ask for a better spot to make camp. Shermon had Dakota and Logon help him count the beef. All three counted 317 head of cattle. Shermon said that is real good. We are within a week of being to Eldorado so we might pick up a couple more but once we get closer to Eldorado there wont be anymore strays or anyway unbranded ones.

They had a real good supper of deer meat with beans, biscuits and black coffee. Shermon said, Cap you out did yourself then Shermon said, lets set up night guard and get some shut eye. Wes Montana said, we sure have a good view, so I think it would be real hard for anyone to sneak up on us. The next morning, they had a quick but good breakfast. Shermon said, Lets head out. So, after the cowboys picked up only 12 more head of cattle on the next days to Eldorado Shermon said, We have 329 beefs and that's real good men.

Shermon told Wes Montana and the rest of the cowboys he would meet them down at the watering hole/steak house in a little while. Dakota you and Logon come with me and let's see what we can get for these beefs. With the 329 beefs the buyers did there best to buy the two young bulls. Shermon said, he would not sell the two young bulls. He needed them to start a new breed of beefs at his ranch Autumn's Crossing. Shermon said, he would accept the thirty-three dollars a head for the 329 head with the total of ten thousand, eight hundred fifty seven dollars. Again, Shermon said, Sorry men the two young bulls are not for sale, like I told you earlier. But I would like to have a bank draft for the ten thousand, eight hundred, fifty seven dollars that we agreed on for the 329 head of beef, plus I will buy you both a steak supper at the place down the street if you will let me. They agreed to Shermon's offer and Shermon, Dakota, Logon and the two buyers walked towards the Watering Hole plus good steakhouse, which is what the sign read.

When they entered the saloon Shermon seen Dakota and Logon both smile at one another. Wes Montana and Cap was sitting at a table and Blacky, Sundance and Nevada were sitting at the bar. Shermon asked the two buyers if they thought it would be okay if they pulled a couple tables together. The one buyer called to Johnny West and told Shermon that Johnny and Ronda West owned the Watering hole. They shook hands and Shermon ordered 10 large steaks with the trimmings then a black coffee with two soda pops.

While waiting for their steaks, Dakota and Logon was taking in all the sites
and smells. Shermon knew that Dakota and Logon had never been in a saloon
before, but it was known for its steaks and he thought that it would be okay as
long as they were there for the steaks only. He also felt that Dakota and Logon
had earned their place at the table. The steaks came with all the fixings with
two soda pops and black coffee for everyone else. Shermon told Johnny and
Ronda West that there sign was right when it said plus a good steak house and
not only a watering hole. They all shook hands and Shermon paid the tally
and said one more time how good the steaks were, and he would be back again
some day. Shermon then said, Kid, lets get them two bulls and head out of
town a ways before we make camp for the night. They were all pretty full and
ready to hit their bed rolls and after a few miles from town they did.

Shermon said, I know we are all ready to get back to Autumn's Crossing
but remember we have a job to do. The better we do on the way to the Ranch
the better for all in the future. We need to take back all the mustang mares and
at least a couple stallions. Plus, we need to pick up all the cows we can for our
two young bulls. Shermon said, the weather looks good and I have not seen
any signs of Indians. We have the two young bulls and 8 long horns. We have
the two young stallions and a few Mustang mares. So, lets see what else we
can pick up on the way back to Autumn's Crossing.

Later that eveinging at the camp, Shermon said, Logon it looks like you
have taken a fancy to that painted stallion? Logon said, Uncle sherm, I think
he is the best horse ever. Shermon said, Logon if you would consider me
breeding him to four or five quarter horse mares we will castrate him and then
you can work to make him your horse. Logon said, thank you, Uncle Sherm!
I will do my best to make him the best horse I can. Shermon said, I know you
will Logon.

Later that day Shermon spotted the white stallion with 20 mares. Wes
Montana said, for a young stallion he sure has a brood of mares. Shermon
said, let's make camp before it gets dark. Let's hope those horses stop up
ahead for the night and then Shermon said, I'm sure they will, we will pick
them up in the morning. Shermon said, we did a good job so far. We have the
two young bulls and 12 Longhorns, plus the two young stallions, in the morning we will go after the white stallion and his 20 mares.

The next morning Shermon asked how all the cowboys were doing? He
didn't want to single out Dakota and Logon. Let's eat and break camp, if ev-

erybody is ready to get closer to Autumn's Crossing. Cap asked Shermon, if salted smoked bacon and biscuits would be okay with coffee. Shermon said, yea save the beans for supper. That morning they finally got two ropes on the white stallion. The Stallion got a lot easier to handle when his 20 mares stayed with him. Shermon said keep those two young stallions away from the white stallion and his mares.

That evening Shermon said, he thought they were only two weeks from home and if the weather stays good and we avoid trouble we should have a good trail. We avoided the trees with the bears and we picked up eight more longhorns, so let's get some shut eye. We need to set up night guard and stay alert Shermon said, and the rest of us let's try to get some rest and then we will pick up what we can in the next days.

Shermon said a couple days later I know we are all feeling the trail and we are thinking of home. But we need to watch for cows and horses plus watch for Indians. I have seen a couple signs of Indians, said Shermon. I don't want to alarm anyone, but we are gathering a few head of cows and some horses and the Indians know we are. We don't want to lose them. We are probably only one week from Autumn's Crossing. And if we are being followed like I think we are they will make a move on us in the next couple of days.

That night Shermon asked, Wes Montana, to stay close to Logon and he would stay close to Dakota. Later that night buck brought his head up and his ears went back, and his nostrils flared. Then Shermon rolled Dakota out of his bedroll. Shermon whispered, put your back to that tree and have your gun ready. Dakota was standing with his back to the tree when he noticed he didn't have his boots on. But Dakota was a little nervous and figured that his uncle rolled him out because of Indians. While Dakota had his back to the tree and not trying to breathe to loud he heard a twig, or something break then he heard another noise. Then Dakota seen the biggest man he had every seen sneak by him.

Then Dakota seen Shermon and his Uncle Whispered, don't move!! Then less than a minute later Dakota seen Shermon put his .44 to the back of the very large mans head. He heard Shermon say drop that rifle or I will send you to an early grave. About the same time Kid Montana had his gun on the large man and said, don't you know better than to sneak into a sleeping camp? The large man said, hold on a minute, Shermon, don't you recognize me? I'm Jack Turner, I came to warn you all. Shermon said, you are lucky that one of us didn't just shoot you. You know better than to walk into a dark camp. But what do you mean warn us? Warn us about what? The large mountain main said, if you give me a chance, I will tell you why I am here.

I went to Eldorado right after you and your cowboys left. Then I seen 10 drifters making plans to ambush you all on the trail. They said they were going to rob you of all your money, plus take all your animals. Wes Montana said, they would have to kill everyone of us to do that. The Large Mountain man said, they are planning on that also. Wes said, why should we believe you? Have you forgot the whipping that you got from Shermon? Jack turner said, Kid you know me. Anyone that can whip me in a fair fight needs to be warned about whats up ahead.

Shermon asked, Turner do you know where they are planning to ambush us? Jack Turner said, they are holed up about half of a mile up ahead. We know right where they are.

Then Jack Tuner said, Shermon I want to help you if you will let me? Shermon said, Thanks for the warning but it's not your fight. Turner said, Shermon, I have two more mountain men out there and like me they want to help. I really want to try and make it up to you for being rude to your lady. So Shermon, how do you want to play it? Shermon said, do you know for sure, they are up ahead. Turner said, they said they were going to hit you at the turn off to Mexico. I hate to say this in front of the young ones, but they said they would take everything and leave you all for buzzard bait. Shermon said, well there is ten men out there that is going to die for a few cows and very little money. The money I had wired to my bank in Waco. They have all kind of cows down in Mexico. The horses are wild and wont trail easy. I have very little cash on me.

Shermon then said, I have no use for any man that trys to ambush another man. So, I am going to ride in and hope to send them all to their graves. Wes Montana said, Sherm, I am riding with you. Shermon said, I will not ask anyone to ride with me. Sundance said, Shermon, me, Nevada and Blacky all ride for the brand, so we will be riding with you for good or bad. Then again, Jack turner said, Shermon I have two lunk heads out there and they are born fighters and they are ready. Shermon said, we have maybe a little over an hour before sunup. I want to hit them before their bed rolls get cold. Blacky said, Sherm, I have a new gun that I just cleaned, and I need to see how it shoots. Shermon said, Nevada and Sundance, I want you two to stay behind with Cap, Dakota and Logon. Then you five start out at sun up. Stay away from the gun play, if possible. Keep the animals together and stay to that ridge over there. We will catch up with you all when this is over. Shermon said, Okay, Jack turner, go get your two friends. Myself, Kid and Blacky will meet you all in about five minutes. Shermon shook hands with Cap, Nevada and Sundance. Then Shermon shook hands with Dakota and Logon.

Chapter 21
The Cowboys with the 3 Mountain men do what needs to be done

So, Cap, with Sundance, Nevada, Logon and Dakota broke camp and started moving the horses and cattle towards the ridge. Shermon, Kid Montana and Blacky headed out with Jack Turner to meet up with the other two mountain men. Wes had just said there goes Cap with the horses and cattle, they are almost to the ridge. Then two large men came towards them and Wes Montana said, I could smell them two before I seen them, if you know what I mean, Shermon! Shermon said, yea, buck had just blown threw his nostrils and had even stamped his feet a couple times before the two mountain men left their cover of the trees. Jack Turner then asked, Shermon how do you want to take them? They came hunting trouble Shermon said. So, lets not waste time talking. We go in and shoot to kill because I don't want to be looking over my shoulder the rest of my life and I can't cotton to anyone that lays in hiding to do their killing. Anyone can shoot a gun, but not many will stand in front of you when you are shooting back at them.

Shermon said, Wes, Blacky and you will go in with me and your two men can hold back a little and watch for any drifters that might slip past us. Don't look into the fire when we get there. Look for green horns laying next to the fire. They probably wont even have a night guard, but they will come up shooting as they roll out of their bedrolls. As Shermon and Wes walked into the camp at the right side of the fire. Jack Turner and Blacky walked in a little to the left of the fire. Shermon said, Kid I count seven men at that fire, so watch for night guards. Next Shermon yelled, Hello in the Camp!!! And as Shermon had said earlier as the drifters rolled out from their blankets they were firing their guns. Wes Montana had two guns already drawn and he was firing them both the same as Shermon was firing his two .44 colts. Blacky was down Shermon knew that Jack Turner had been shot atleast once, but the mountain man was standing tall and he had a level action 44 spencer rifle and he knew how to use it. So, when the shooting stopped, and the smoke cleared the sun was coming up.

There was six dead men by the fire and one dying. Shermon asked, Jack Turner who was leaning against a tree, how he was doing? Turner said, I'm still standing but I got hit two different times. I think your man Blacky pulled an empty gun. Shermon said, an empty gun, what do you mean by that? The big mountain man said, I was standing right next to him and the first thing I heard was click....click. His hammer was hitting on empty chambers that's what I mean.

The only drifter still alive was crying over by the fire. I don't want to die. Kid, check on Blacky and bring me his gun, while I deal with this coward, Shermon said and see how bad Turner is shot. As Shermon went over to the man on the ground, Shermons eyes were cold he had a look on him that would sour milk. Again, the drifter cried .... I don't want to die. Shermon said, then you should not have come looking for trouble. You are going to die Shermon said, but it is up to you how you die. You can lay here gut shot and wait to die, or you can put a bullet in your head and end the suffering.

But first I see three sets of tracks that left this camp not too long ago so I if you tell me about the tracks, I will see if I can help you. No sooner than the words came out of Shermon's mouth, the drifter said the tracks are Tyrell Morgan and his brother Trent, plus the third is just a drifter that said that all he wanted was to see Tyrell Morgan give you the beating that you deserve. The the dying cowboy said, you said you would help me. As Jack Turner's two mountain men came into camp they saw Shermon hand the drifter the gun that he had dropped in the dirt earlier when he was first shot crawling out of his blanket. You are dying Shermon said, so like I said earlier you can lay here gut shot and die slow and painfully or you can end it now and rot in hell. The cowboy closed his eyes and with the gun to his head he pulled the trigger as everyone watched, except Blacky, because Blacky was also dead.

One of the mountain men said, Jack your friend sure has a streak of meanness in him, don't he? Shermon looked at the mountain man and said, they were all violent men, they came to kill, they were all a salty lot and now they will be in unmarked graves. Jack Turner then asked, What about their horses and gear? Shermon said, Jack Turner, I thank you for your help you and your two friends can have their horses, gear and whatever else you find in their saddle bags. Wes Montana said, Shermon, Blacky's gun was empty and I believe he knew it. Shermon looked at Blacky's gun and then looked at Blacky. Blacky had been shot in the chest twice. They heard a shot fired. Shermon said, sounds like they have caught up with Cap and the rest. Let's roll Blacky up in his bedroll and tie him to his horse. Then Shermon said, Jack Turner, if you and your two friends will take care of these cowards you three can have their horses, saddles and whatever else you find here. Jack Turner shook hands with Shermon and Wes Montana. Shermon said, I'm sure I will see you again. The mountain man said, I'm sure you will friend. Also, be real careful when you reach your chuck wagon. Shermon said, they would. Then said, I hope your gun wounds aren't bad. The mountain man said, I've cut myself worse trying to shave. Then there were three shots together. Shermon said, lets ride kid.

As they rode off, Wes Montana looked back and the three mountain men were starting to strip the seven dead men. Shermon heard Jack Turner say don't leave anything for the bears or wolves. The three mountain men took everything except their clothes, because the clothes were of course too small for the three Large mountain men. So, they burned the clothes in the fire with the seven dead men. Turner said, lets ride over to where we heard the gun fire because right now, these seven smells worse then you two. The mountain men had the seven horses of the seven dead men, plus their guns, saddles and saddle bags plus even a little money that they took off the dead men. Jack Turners leg had started bleeding a little again where the bullet had gone threw but the so called scratch on his forehead was just another ugly mark to go with the rest of the scars on his face.

The three mountain men were very quiet for as big as they were but they could not hide the foul smell that they took with them wherever they went. Jack Turner and his two large friends snuck right up on the three men that held

Shermon and his cowboys at gun point. Wes Montana smelled them first and looked over at Shermon. Tyrell Morgan had just brought his big right hand back to hit Shermon again, Shermon yelled, HIT THE DIRT!!!! Dakota and Logon both dropped to the ground then both Jack Turners friends each stuck a gun to both off Tyrell's friends' heads. Jack Turner said, if they move, kill them!!

Jack Turner had his gun against the back of Tyrell Morgan's head. The mountain man said, if any of you feel lucky try anything and none of you three will see another sunrise. Then Jack Turner said, Shermon this big jug head had a couple free shots at you. Are you up to teaching him a lesson or two? Shermon said, yea, as he brought a long right that looked like it was brought from the ground to Tyrell Morgan's nose, blood squirted everywhere. Morgan yelled, you broke my nose again!! Then Shermon threw a combination of a left cross to the right side of Morgan's head and then a right hook to the left side of Morgan's head. That would have stopped most men, but Tyrell Morgan took a couple steps back and then charged Shermon. Shermon stepped to his right and hit Morgan in the throat and then Morgan took his last breath looking up at Shermon.Shermon buckeled his colts back on.

Shermon looked at Kid and said we had a good cowboy get killed tonight because of these two plus I won't have anyone hold guns on my nephews for any reason. I don't think we will let you two just ride out, you both have big mouths and I sure don't want to be looking over my backside from now on to see if one or both of you are behind me. Trent Morgan said, I won't fight you, but I think I am faster with a gun than Kid Montana is. The guy with Trent Morgan said, yea Kid, your reputation doesn't scare me either and they both laughed. Wes Montana said, give them both their guns back and we will find out who is faster. Shermon said, Kid I will stand with you.

But Kid Montana said, Shermon you whipped big Tyrell Morgan like you were just walking over short grass. Let me stand in front of these two. Sundance and Nevada said, do it for Blacky, Kid. Kid Montana said, hand them their guns. So Shermon handed the cowboys their guns and the three mountain men watched on as Kid Montana stood in front of Trent Morgan and his friend. Wes Montana said, whenever you are ready to die, slap leather boys!! You could see Trrent and his friend was starting to wonder if they should have thought it over a little more. But then Wes winked at them and they both went for their guns. Kid Montana pulled both of his .44's and put a bullet in the heart of each man. When they fell neither one had cleared their holsters. Wes Montana said, that was for you, Blacky Moore.

Jack Turner said, to his two friends, did you ever see anyone faster with a gun? They both said, no that they never had seen a faster gun. They also said they were sorry to say it, but they knew why their frind Jack Turner got beat by Shermon, after seeing the beating that Shermon gave to Tyrell Morgan. Jack Turner told Shermon that the three of them had all the excitement that they could handle for one day. Shermon said, hey, Big Jack or if it's okay I will call you B.J.? Jack Turner said, Shermon you earned it, B.J. is fine with me. Shermon said, you can have the three horses and saddles, but I think Kid earned the guns, okay? B.J. said that's fine with us three and Shermon that sure was a hell of a fight you put on. Shermon said, well B.J., I believe that it's not the fight that you are in but it's the fight that's in you.

B.J. and the other two mountain men took the three horses and the three saddles but threw the saddle bags and bedrolls on the ground next to the chuck-wagon. Shermon then shook hands with Wes Montana and said that he was glad that they were on the same side. Wes Montana said, Shermon you do have a mean streak in you and I am also glad we are on the same side. Shermon shook Cap Preston's hand and looked at Dakota and Logon. He walked over to them and as he shook their hands he asked how they were doing? Dakota and Logon both said they were fine, then Dakota said, Uncle Sherm, me and Logon also now know what they mean when they say you have a mean streak. Logon said, yea Uncle Sherm, like Wes Montana said, you walked threw that guy Tyrell Morgan like you were walking through short grass.

Dakota and Logon both said that they had never seen such a fight. Then they said, and we never seen a gun fight before either. Kid you were very good and very fast, Shermon said, both the gun fight and me ending Morgan's life could not be avoided. It's not something that you look forward to sometimes you must play the cards you are dealt you can't always walk away but fighting is not the only way to win. Sometimes it is walking away or avoiding an unneccesary fight that makes you win Dakota and Logon both said, we understand if you have to fight, fight to win. Shermon smiled at his nephews.

Then he shook hands with Sundance and Nevada. Shermon asked do one of you know why Blacky's gun was empty? Then Cap said, boss here is a note that he left with your name on it. Shermon took the paper and read it out loud.

Shermon,

I sure did enjoy the time I spent with you and your family. I also enjoyed being with all the cowboys. I have been hurting real bad. The pain was getting to hard to live with. I am sorry, but I did not tell you because the doctor I seen said there was nothing he could do. I would have been 40 my next birthday. Sherm, will you give Cap my horse and saddle because I think every cowboy should have their own horse. My horse, or Caps horse will answer to Pepper. I named him Pepper when he was just a colt. Sherm, will you keep my Colt .44, I just cleaned it for you, it has a hair trigger. I will see you all in the here after. Thanks everyone.

    Blacky

Chapter 22
Shermon and his Cowboys head
to Autumn's Crossing

Shermon said Cap you can have pepper your new horse when we reach Autumn's Crossing but for now if you will put the saddle and this Colt in the chuck wagon. We will bury Blacky on that little knoll over there under the large oak tree. Dakota will you and Logon build a cross? Sundance you and Nevada dig a hole and we will place the cross on the hole after we bury Blacky. Shermon said, let me say a few words for Blacky, then we will head out. They were all quiet as they rode away. Shermon did say, I haven't seen any Indian signs plus the weather is real good.

Three days later Shermon said, the line shack is just up ahead. Harry and Mario Austin waved to them as they were moving the horses and cows towards the line shack. Then later Harry told Shermon that he knew something was hurting in Blacky. Harry said, I tried to talk with him but Blacky said talking would not help. Mario was saying how good the two young bulls looked also the mustangs. But the white stallion was not happy here. Dakota said that White one will get use to it, because he will be mine as soon as Uncle Sherm says so. Logon said, you see that painted one Mario, when Uncle Sherm says so, he will be mine. Mario said, well looks like you two will have your jobs cut out for you with those two. Dakota said, Uncle Sherm said we will have to earn their trust, then with them being castrated they will tame down pretty quick. Well if I can help, let me know Mario said.

Sherm said, we really want to get back so if you all have any extra jerky and a couple biscuits we will eat it on the way back to the ranch. Harry said, that they had plenty to spare and asked Mario to fix up seven go orders. Cap told Harry that Blacky had left him Pepper in a note to Shermon and that would be his very first horse of his own. Blacky said, every man needs his own horse. Harry said that Blacky was right about that. But then he said, I've seen you on many horses before. Cap said, yes, but they always belonged to someone else normally, whoever I was working for at the time. Mario came up with Seven sacks with Jerky and 2 biscuits in each sack, plus he had a large water jug in which they all filled their canteens. Shermon said, you cowboys ready? Let's roll.

They ate in the saddle and pushed the horses and beef towards the ranch. It wasn't very long until they were at the ranch. They pushed the beef in a large 3 strand fence and then divided the four stallions, the two young colts then the white one with his mare's then the painted stallion with his mares in the last holding corral. Then Shermon sat on buck and looked around like he did so often. There had been a lot done while he and his cowboys were on the trail. Abigail was hugging Logon and Brandy was hugging Dakota, plus Lance and Wyatt was giving the two young men a look that only a proud father could give a son. Then the two women hugged Shermon and as Lance and Wyatt was shaking hands with Shermon, KaSandra and Reminton came around from the other side of the ranch house.

Reminton came up and shook Shermons hand then Dakotas and Logons and said Sherm, looks like you are short one cowboy. Shermon said, yea Blacky did not make it back, we ran into some trouble and we buried Blacky under a large oak tree on a small hillside. KaSandra came up and hugged Shermon and said, it looks like you have some new bruises, are you going to tell us what happened? Let's have some coffee and I will tell you everything after I knock some of this dust off. But first I want to know how everything went here while I was gone on the trail, plus where is Cheyenne? Kasandra said, Cheyenne should be back anytime and as you can see we got a lot done while you cowboys where on the trail.

Just then Cheyenne rode into Autumn's Crossing and dove off her horse buttons and right into Shermons arms. They kiss a good long kiss and Cheyenne asked Shermon if he missed her. Shermon said, everyday and every night. Cheyenne said, Good, Big man, but it looks like you have some new bruises. Yes, I do have some new bruises. We run into some trouble on the way back and Cheyenne, we buried Blacky under a large oak tree on a hillside. He was shot and killed. Cheyenne felt real bad about Blacky being killed. She knew Blacky Moore for more than 10 years the same as Luther Green. Blacky stayed to himself for the most part but he was always a kind man and told Cheyenne more than once if she ever needed his help that he would be there for her. So, what happened Sherm? Abigail said, theres coffee and Brandy is bringing smoked ham and biscuits.

Let's go over and get in the shade and I will tell you about our trail drive. Shermon called Wes Montana, Sundance and Nevada over because Cap, Dakota and Logon plus Luther was already at the dinner table. KaSandra then brought over a jug of sun tea which Dakota and Logon was happy to see. The rest of the cowboys drank coffee and said, it was the best coffee they had in awhile, not that Cap's wasn't good, but they mostly drank Cap's coffee while they were in the saddle.

Chapter 23
They tell the story of the trail drive

Shermon started by saying we made it to Eldorado with 329 beefs without much trouble we sold our beefs for a good price and then we had a good steak dinner with all the trimmings at a place called the watering hole plus a good steak house. Believe me it was a good steak house. The coffee was good but a couple of us had soda pops. Dakota and Logon both grinned and then Dakota asked where is Lexie, Katelyn and Valerie? Abigail said, they are at the school house with Dawn Marie the school mom, they will be home soon. Then Abigail said, go ahead Sherm and tell us everything.

Well I got a bank note at the Eldorado bank and had the money wired to the bank here in Waco. There was a lot of drifters in Eldorado and I just thought it would be the right thing to do. So, after we left Eldorado, you remember the mountain man Jack Turner? Cheyenne said, I sure do, and I can't believe he wanted anymore trouble from you Shermon. No, it wasn't that Shermon said, but he heard some drifters in town talking about ambushing us and he with two other large mountain men came to warn us and help if they could.

Dakota said, that's right me and Uncle Sherm was on night watch when Uncle Sherm shook me awake and had me stand behind a tree and that's when the biggest man I ever seen snuck by me towards our camp fire. Wes Montana said, Dakota you said, Sherm shook you awake, I thought you first said you were on night watch with Sherm and laughed. Well I guess I dozed off for a

minute. Shermon said, you did good Dakota. Anyway, then I came up behind
B.J. and put my gun barrell behind his ear and said, I would think you know
better to walk into a camp at night and not even call our first. Then B.J. said,
he had come to warn me about some drifters who he heard talking in town that
they were going to ambush us before we got back to Autumn's Crossing. B.J.
said, they had plans of getting the cattle money and drive our horses and beef
to Mexico. That's the reason we were only about three days from Autumns
Crossing. They wanted us to pick up all the horses and cows and then they
were going to hit us and take whatever horses, cows and money we had and
turn towards Mexico. So, we did all the work and they thought they would
have a straight shot to Mexico. KaSandra asked, Sherm why do you call the
big mountain man B. J. if his name is Jack Turner? The B is for Big and the
J is for Jack. And I'm sure someday you all will meet B.J. and see how big
mountain man Jack Turner is anyway the ones that have not seen B.J yet.

Cheyenne then said, Shermon I'm still a little surprised that Jack Turner
warned you. Cheyenne, B.J. said, he was sorry about being rude to you that
day and wanted to make it up to us after the whipping he received from me.
Anyway, Kid, Blacky and I went with B.J. and met his two friends up the trail.
Wes Montana said, yea we smelled his friends before we seen them leave the
tree line. Dakota and Logon both said, yea them two big mountain men sure
did have a stink about them. So, what happened Sherm? Reminton asked.
Well Kid and I walked up to their fire from the left side and Blacky and B.J.
walked up to the fire from the right side. I had asked B.J.'s two friends to stay
back and watch the trail in case someone made a run for it. We walked into
their camp, I said, "Wake up you cowards" and they came up with their guns
blazing. We shot and killed 6 of the 7 men laying around the fire when they
jumped up. The seventh man was gut shot and dying but before he died he said
Tyrell and Trent Morgan plus a friend left and he was pretty sure that they were
headed for our chuck wagon.

Cheyenne, Blacky's gun wasn't even loaded. What do you mean Sherm,
Cheyenne asked? He left me a note and I have it here. Blacky said he was in
pain from his stomach and he hoped to draw their gun fire to him and away
from us, then Shermon handed the note to Cheyenne. Cheyenne said, that sure
sounds like Blacky and this note said he cleaned his Colt .44 for you and gave
his horse and saddle to Cap. That also sounds like Blacky. Then what Sherm,
Reminton asked? I told B.J. that he and his two friends could have the horses

and saddles and whatever else the seven drifters or cowards had and take care of their bodys. We headed towards the shots. Tyrell Morgan had Cap shoot three times because he knew that would bring us fast. But when we got there Trent Morgan and the other drifter friend of his had their two guns held on Dakota and Logon so Tyrell took a couple free shots at me with his fist. Then B.J.'s two friends stuck their guns on Trent and his friend and took their guns after that B.J. said, Sherm this here lunk head is yours if you want him. Before B.J. got the words out of his mouth I broke Morgans Jaw, his nose and stuck my bowie in Morgans heart after busting his throat. Dakota and Logon said you guys should have seen it. Uncle Sherm has a mean streak in him and he walked over Morgan like he was walking over short grass. Cheyenne said, that's right big man, you do have a mean streak in you. KaSandra said, it's not Shermons fault he just can't tolerate rude people. And Reminton said, he just can't cotton to it. Shermon said, Okay, I think that's enough and they all laughed.

Then Trent and his drifter friend thought they wanted Kids quick draw title. Dakota said, you should have seen Kid draw both of his guns at one time and shoot both men in their hearts at the same time. Wes Montana then said, Dakota, I would like to say right now the reason I had to kill those two men is because of my reputation. Dakota said, you and Uncle Sherm both said they all came hunting trouble and we gave it to them Kid. Shermon then said, Dakota, what Kid means is once you draw against anyone it's probally the start of many more to come because there is a whole lot of young guns out there trying to make a name for themselves. So, if you have a repuation with a gun you could find yourself looking over your shoulder or into the barrel of some other cowboys' gun for the rest of your life. Dakota said, Mario said, he would teach me how to quick draw if it was okay. Don't rush it Dakota, Wes Montana said. Because anyone can learn to draw a gun fast or to shoot a gun fast but the real thing is how you act when you are being shot at. Dakota said, I know what you mean and I'm not looking to have a gun fight, but I want to be able to handle a gun and to handle it fast if I need too. Shermon said, I think every man and every woman that wants to should know how to handle a gun and also a rope plus I think Mario would be a good one to show you when the time is right.

Okay, we had a long trail drive and we will take tomorrow off but theres more building to do and we have plenty of horses to break and cattle to brand so whoever wants to hit the sack or just take a break before hitting the sack go for it. Pay time will be tomorrow after breakfast. Now Reminton if you will get your tally book or ledger I have some numbers for you to put in it. First Reminton, what is the number you have now for our grand total? Reminton said, it is thirty thousand, eight hundred, eighty dollars after the bank draft we wrote for the other three thousand, two hundred acres which the draft was for Two thousand, five hundred dollars which I have the receipt right here and the title is also here with the title for our original six thousand, four hundred acres.

Okay Shermon said, we took 329 beef to Eldorado and I have a bank note here for ten thousand, eight hundred, ten dollars which comes to what is the total you have now Reminton, Shermon Asked? The total that I have is forty-one thousand, six hundred, ninety dollars that's real good Shermon said, and we have a working ranch now. Reminton, tomorrow after breakfast I want us to make a payroll first for the cowboys which includes Cap, Shorty, Dakota and Logon. Thirty dollars each for our foreman Wes Montana his Sixty dollars then we have Sundance, Nevada, Luther, Shane, Harry, Mario and Jesse each of their fifty dollars and found for them all and your total is five hundred, thirty dollars monthly pay and found so deduct that and your total is forty-one thousand, one hundred, sixty dollars.

Reminton, Arthur Travis the President of Waco's bank talked to me about make a deposit in his bank. Art told me that if we deposited ten thousand dollars or more at his bank not only would we be his largest depositer but for ten thousand dollars or more he would pay us 3% back on our money every month for letting him use our money. So, I was thinking if we let him use twenty thousand dollars of our money that would give us six hundred dollars a month back which would pay our payroll plus fifty dollars a month that could be used at the general store. Reminton said, I knew Art was busy making a lot of loans. The town is really growing. Well Art told me he was having to borrow a lot of money from a couple other banks and he is paying 4% to use their money so it just seems good for Art to use our money and for us to let him use it then us pay our payroll through the bank. Art said he would make all the payouts the first of every month if we wanted to give him enough cash to do so. Lance and Wyatt were sitting at the table so Shermon said, what do you two, think? We all have a stake in this, so we all have a say. So, Lance what do you and Wyatt think?

Lance said, I think it almost sounds to good, and Wyatt agreed with Lance. Not really, Reminton said, Waco's bank is paying other banks to use their money and there's more money for Arthur to make if he used our money. Wyatt said, Well Sherm, this is why you and Rem have been handling the money and making deals. I will run the sawmill until you decide that I am needed somewhere else. Shermon said, Wyatt now that you brought that up. I think after we build all or most of what we are going to build, we will stock pile some fence post and sell the saw mill for a good profit. How would you like to work in the blacksmith shop? I think you and Lance would make a good team. Lance said, I like that ideal if you do Wyatt? Wyatt said, it would be closer to home and laughed, I'll do it Sherm. Then it's agreed to put twenty thousand dollars in Waco's bank and Reminton you follow up with Art on all transactions.

So, lets see how much we need to add to the bank draft of ten thousand, eight hundred, ten dollars. Reminton said if we add nine thousand, one hundred, ninety dollars to the ten thousand, eight hundred, ten dollars that will give us the twenty thousand dollars. Then we will receive 3% on our twenty thousand dollars which will be six hundred dollars. That will take care of payroll, plus fifty dollars a month to be used at the general store if needed. Shermon said, so what do we have in the cash box? We have two land deeds, the original six thousand, four hundred acres and then the three thousand, two hundred acres plus letters and papers. Then we will have twenty-one thousand, one hundred, sixty dollars in large bills, after our meeting with Arthur Travis Tomorrow. Shermon said, Rem, if you will put that cash box back in the safe, we will ride into town in the morning.

Cheyenne asked, hey big man, can me and KaSandra ride into town in the morning with our two cowboys? Shermon said, me and Rem, would love for you two to ride into town with us. Other than the bank, we do have a couple other stops to make Shermon said. KaSandra said, we have all day Cheyenne said, yea, big man don't worry about us. Then Shermon said, Lance why don't you and Wyatt walk over to the black smith shop with me. I would really like to see how far it is, then I believe I will be ready for some Shut eye. Lance said, I would like for you to see it. But remember it is only a shell right now. Wyatt said, we wanted your input on the tack room and loft. So now is a good time to look at it.

When they walked inside, Shermon looked around. Shermon was smiling and said, I am really pleased with the size of this large building. Also, the way you laid this out. Lance asked, how do you think we should run the loft? Well

I would like to see the loft run from end to end, with a walkway from side to side. Then have a ladder at all four ends with a rope and pulley at all four ladders. Have the tack room on one side in the center with maybe five horse stalls on either side then across on the other side. Have eight single stalls and two or three double stalls that can be four or six singles. Those four or six stalls will be because of removable dividers that could be put in for single stalls or removed for double stalls if needed. Wyatt asked, Shermon, do you think we will need 20 or more horse stalls?   Shermon said, Wyatt, we need to look at the big picture. We have the room so why not use it. Remember it's better to have them and not need them, then to need them and not have them. Wyatt said, I see what you mean now. Lance with all the open area you and Wyatt will have you will be able to work on wagons or on small horse shoes. There wll be plenty of loft area for storage. I would like to have hay storage mostly on the outside of the blacksmith shop. We will build a hay storage shelter for whatever hay we might want to store Shermon said.

Now for a very important thing, that I think we should have. I hope we will never have to use it, but I think we should have a false ceiling in the tack room with a ladder to the loft. Always have a couple guns and ammo handy. Then also have an escape hatch in the roof with a ladder from the loft to the roof. Again, I will say I really hope we don't ever have to use it. We will only let our family and our cowboys that ride for the brand know about this. Lance said, Sherm you sure have put a lot of thought into this haven't you? Shermon said, well Lance as you know I spent more than two years of my life with the apaches. I had plenty of time to think. So, all I thought of was other than escaping was my family and this ranch. After we complete this blacksmith shop then we will have the Gun way to build. Also, a good size chicken coop with an enclosed fence for chickens and eggs. The women even said they would help with the netting to keep the chickens safe. Wyatt, once we get to the point of selling the sawmill you will help Lance operate the blacksmith shop. It will be yours and Lance's operation and also running the shop. There will be many items to make and care for here at Autumn's Crossing plus any free time will be yours and Lance's if theres available time the two of you can do jobs for cash or trade for town people or others.   The gun way will sell new and used guns plus ammo plus work on guns. Shermon said, I think I need some shut eye. I'm really tired and I'm sure you are too. He shook his brothers' hands and said I am so happy with all we have done so far. I'm proud of my family and our cowboys. We have a lot to do tomorrow. This is only the start of good things to come.

Reminton was standing by the bunk house as Shermon, Lance and Wyatt walked up. Luther and Sundance were singing a soft country song with Harry and Nevada, plus Mario picking a guitar and singing along with them. Shermon said to his brothers the only voice missing was Blacky's low voice. Kid Montana said, Cap was out here singing earlier but then he started thinking about Blacky, I guess and went inside. Shermon said, I wanted to stop by and tell you Kid, plus the other cowboys, as this place grows with all our hard work. I promise you all that we will grow and so will all of you. I want to thank everyone of you for all the hard work and for riding for the brand. I know that Jesse and Shane are at the line shack, so I will tell them what I just said when I see them.

As Shermon and his three brothers walked towards the large ranch house. The four women were sitting on the long porch enjoying the singing cowboys. KaSandra said, them cowboys sure sing and play well. But I wish they would sing something that was not so sad and lonely. Shermon said, well KaSandra most cowboys are lonely and lead a sad life. But most cowboys pick the life that they live. Cheyenne said, Sherm, I wanted to ask you, you said earlier that the guy you had to kill on the trail was Tyrell Morgan, right? Shermon said, yes, that's right. So, the big guy you whipped in Eldorado was the same coward that you had to kill on the trail? Shermon said, That's right. He attacked you in elderado and I had to whip him, then I had to whip him again on the trail plus kill him because he pulled a jack knife on me. That's when I put my bowie threw his heart. So, he won't attack any other woman again. I told him that I would kill him, and he made me keep my promise. Also, Kid got a real nice pocket knife because Morgan won't need it any more.

Chapter 24
Shermon and Cheyenne set the date

October 15th, 1850

Shermon said, Cheyenne Decker, I would like to make you an honest woman. Shermon said, how about October 15th, 1850? We left Kansas City, Missouri on October 15th, 1848, and I think October 15th, 1850 would be a great time to tie the knot. Cheyenne was crying but she said, Big Man I told you I would be ready when you were ready to marry me. All four women were crying and even the three girls were crying. Shermon said look I made everyone cry, I'm sorry. Cheyenne said, don't be sorry we are all happy. Shermon and Cheyenne kissed and hugged and everyone else stood in line to hug Shermon and Cheyenne. Even the cowboys all walked over to the ranch house to congratulate Shermon and Cheyenne. Shermon said, we will have the wedding here at Autumn's Crossing. KaSandra said, Cheyenne we have so much to get ready in only four months. Cheyenne asked KaSandra to be her Bridesmaid. Cheyenne said, I would like for your whole family plus all your cowboys to be in our wedding. Shermon said, whoever you want to be in our wedding is okay by me. Cheyenne said, I would like to see my sister and have her here for our wedding. Shermon said, Cheyenne, I am sorry, I didn't even ask about your family. Of course, your whole family is invited to our wedding. Well Sherm, I have a brother and a sister but I only want to invite my sister Maxine is her name, but I mostly call her Tennessee since she moved to Tennessee.

Cheyenne your sister can come as soon as she can and stay with us for as long as she wants before and after our wedding. Plus, your brother is also welcome if you would want to contact him, I can help you find him if you want me to? Sherm, my sister is good, and I would enjoy spending time with her and I thank you for that. But as far as my brother Keith, he goes by the name of Ace Angel and he is very bad, and I know you don't know it right now, but he is very dangerous and has done some bad things. I know he's not here and that's good. Cheyenne said, Shermon you had better talk with Kid or Harry or even Mario before you think about inviting my brother here now or ever. Shermon said, okay I will talk with them. You get a hold of your sister and tell her there's plenty of room here for her. Tell Maxine we will be looking for her to arrive as soon as she can. Cheyenne said our wedding is 4 months away you tell Maxine we have a large place here and she will have her own room. Tell her she is invited to stay on here as long as she likes. Cheyenne hugged Shermon with tears in her eyes, but she was very happy. Then she said, Sherm you seem awful excited. Shermon said, I am, I'm getting married and your sister is coming. I never wanted to marry before, but I sure do now. Cheyenne said, Big man I never wanted to marry anyone before I met you.

It will be a wedding that everyone will be talking about for a long time. We will invite the whole town. I will ask our cowboys to play their guitars and sing. We will butcher a whole cow plus a whole pig. Also, build a dance floor. Shermon was so excited that he just kept going on and on with ideas for the wedding. No one could believe that Shermon McBay was so excited, but he sure was!!!

Shermon wrote on a piece of paper:

Shermon Robert McBay

and Cheyenne Nicole Decker

Wedding

October 15th, 1850

Autumn's Crossing

Everyone is invited to attend

Shermon looked at Cheyenne tears were running down Cheyenne's face the same as KaSandra's, Brandy's and Abigails. Shermon noticed that his brothers and the cowboys were also sniffing and blowing their noses. Shermon said, look, I did not mean to make everyone cry. Cheyenne said, hey big man, these are happy tears and jumped into Shermon's arms and they kissed.

After hand shakes and hugs, Shermon said, I thank God for today and for Cheyenne and I pray that I can be the husband you deserve. Cheyenne said, I know you will be Shermon Robert McBay.

Then Cheyenne said, tomorrow will be a big day, so let's see if we can get some shut eye and then everyone laughed out loud. Shermon said, I will talk with Kid, Harry and Mario tomorrow about your brother Keith, plus listen to anyone else that has anything to say about this so called Ace Angel. Then they all headed to bed and thanked God for the day they had and for the days to come.

Chapter 25
Everyone is Invited to the Wedding, Except, Ace Angel

The next morning as Shermon was pouring his self a cup of coffee, Wes Montana walked up and said, are you drinking alone, or do you want some company? Shermon said, sit down Kid, I would like to ask you about Keith or Ace Angel. Kid said, he is bad Sherm, very bad! Well Kid, I think I should know about him seeing as how I am marrying his sister, don't you? Wes said, I knew you would hear of him someday, so let me see where to start. Shermon said, start at the beginning that has always worked for me.

Wes Montana then said, you see Sherm, Keith felt like he was an outsider. He never got along with anyone and was always in some type of trouble. When Keith was younger, he would always start trouble but would always end up on the bottom. Then Keith bought his first gun and he practiced all the time. So as Keith got older, he grew not only in size, but he also grew meaner. As the years went by, he practiced with his guns and started winning all his fist fights. Sherm, Keith, fights to win like you do but he is a very dirty fighter and fights to hurt people by all means possible.

Then, Keith took the name, Ace Angel. He throws dirt, sticks his fingers in his opponents' eyes and anything else to win. I was out on a trail drive with some other cowboys. Angel had the drop on Harry and would have killed him, but Mario came up behind Angel and knocked him out cold with his .44 Colt. The Marshall Mountain Mitch put Angel in jail and then released Angel in his dad's care. When Angel's dad got Angel home a fight broke out between Angel and his dad and Sherm, Angel shot and killed his dad. Maxine or Tennessee as they call her, shot at Angel and hit him in his gun hand. But, when Angel rode out of town, he swore to kill Maxine, Harry and Mario someday.

Shermon poured himself and Kid another cup of coffee. Then Shermon asked, Kid, do you think his gun hand has healed, and do you think he will try to make good on his promise? Wes said, Shermon, I know his hand has healed and know he always wears two .44 colts and he is real good with them both. It has been five years, last I heard Angel has been down in Mexico. They have a hide out close to the border.

Sherm, don't take light of Angel, he is running with a real bad lot of cut throats that would shoot their own mom or dad just like Angel did. And I hate to say it, but they would laugh while doing it then rob them as they were dying. Believe me Sherm, there is no one in the town of Waco or here at Autumn's Crossing that would ever want to see Ace Angel come to town again!!! Shermon said, Well Kid there's another reason why we need to be careful and as you said, I hope we don't have to kill Ace Angel and his friends, but we will if pushed.

Shermon picked up the piece of paper that he had wrote the wedding invitation on, which read:

Shermon Robert McBay
and Cheyenne Nicole Decker
Wedding
October 15th, 1850
Autumn's Crossing
Everyone is invited to attend

Then Shermon added:
Except Ace Angel,
And his friends.
They are not invited!!